To Cass

RISING SHADOWS
A WORLD IN SHADOWS · BOOK 1

Let's be Shield buddies! ♥

BRIDGET BLACKWOOD

Bridget Blackwood

To Cass

Let's be
Shield buddies!

Today!
Rockwood

Copyright © 2014 Bridget Jackson

All rights reserved under International and Pan-American Copyright Conventions

By payment of required fees, you have been granted the non-exclusive, non-transferable right to access and read the text of this book. No part of this text may be reproduced, transmitted, downloaded, decompiled, reverse engineered, or stored in or introduced into any information storage and retrieval system, in any form or by any means, whether electronic or mechanical, now known or hereinafter invented without the express written permission of copyright owner.

Please Note

The reverse engineering, uploading, and/or distributing of this book via the internet or via any other means without the permission of the copyright owner is illegal and punishable by law. Please purchase only authorized electronic editions, and do not participate in or encourage electronic piracy of copyrighted materials. Your support of the author's rights is appreciated

No part of this book may be reproduced or transmitted in any form or by any electronic or mechanical means, including photocopying, recording or by any information storage and retrieval system, without the written permission of the publish-er, except where permitted by law.

Cover Design by Kelly Walker

Edited by Samantha Ettinger

This is a work of fiction. Names, characters, places, brands, media, and incidents are either the product of the author's imagination or are used fictitiously. Any resemblance to similarly named places or to persons living or deceased is unintentional.

Acknowledgments

Without God, I wouldn't be where I am today. Thank you for all my blessings.

Beta Babes; Alexandra Bowers, Brandi Gilvaja, Christina McGee, Lindsay Chamberlain. Each of you is a bright star in my sky.

Editors; Samantha Ettinger, Candice Barnes, and Sharon Stogner

Cover Designer; Kelly Walker at Indie-Spired Design

Chelsea Barnes, you're a rock star.

The Black Cats, my reader group on Facebook. You keep me laughing and smiling.

Thanks Katy Regnery and Skhye Moncrief for your advice

My family deserves this dedication because they're dedicated to me.

Mom, I've called you my north star many times because you provide me with a fixed point to navigate through life. Thank you for all the lessons.

My three little squishies. You are my greatest achievement.

John – with you I found forever.

*"Mortal fate is hard.
You'd best get used to it."*

—EURIPIDES, MEDEA

Prologue

Rachel

THEY'RE GOING TO do it again.

Each time they take me into that room I start over. A clean slate. It takes a while for my brain to force the memories back up to the surface, but I can tell I remember less with each procedure.

I feel the absence of my own identity.

You've felt something similar when the word or thought is on the tip of your tongue. Try as hard as you can it stays just out of reach. For me, the distance between memory and oblivion keeps growing wider.

Tomorrow I'll wake up and forget who I am again.

CHAPTER 1

Rachel

I WAKE IN A COLORLESS ROOM, both the tile floor and the walls are white, the glaring lack of color is made noticeable by the sunshine streaming through the bars of a small window above my bed.

Why am I in a room with bars?

An IV pole is pushed against the bed frame and a tube tethers me to the bag via a catheter embedded in my left hand. After peeling off the tape, I gently draw the foreign object from my body. *I hate needles.* My eyes shut, I attempt to remember the last place I was. Nothing. I draw a blank.

Why can't I remember? My scalp is tender; I ache all over. *Was I in a wreck?* My entire body feels beaten. Not debilitating pain, but like the day after a hard workout.

I catch a deep breath and try to stand. After a few tries, I succeed on shaky legs and head for the chart dangling at the foot of the bed.

Patient name: Rachel Ryan.
Age: 24. Caucasian female.
No living relatives.
Agent acquisition on 06/29/2010
Arcana administered 07/07/2010

Testing and results:...

No other information is available to help fill in the blanks. Nothing to explain what Arcana is or how a person becomes an acquisition. I flip through the many test reports stapled together but can't make sense of the medical jargon. Every so often the words *tabula rasa* appear in all caps.

Why do I know that phrase?

I replace the chart with a sigh. The short walk to the door isn't far but takes a lot out of me. Locked. I pull on the door a few times, but it still won't budge.

"Hey! Somebody open the door!" I bang on the door with the flat of my hand but nobody comes. I feel on the verge of an anxiety attack. *Okay, don't panic.* The IV I pulled out must have contained a sedative because I can barely keep my eyes open. Back on the bed I lay down unable to fight whatever they put in my system.

A gentle touch rouses me. There is a woman; tall with fair hair and faded blue eyes. I think she's a nurse. I allow her to inspect my hand where I pulled the IV out. It's amazing how we trust people in uniform. Inmates wear uniforms. If a person walks into your room dressed in an orange jumpsuit with Department of Corrections on the back, you don't get friendly. A woman in scrubs walks in and I'm ready to do anything she asks. She picks up the abandoned IV catheter.

"We inserted this for a purpose," she scolds.

I ignore her attempt to shame me. "Can you tell me how I got here?"

The nurse looks at me bewildered. She grabs my chart and

looks at the last page. Rolling her eyes and scoffing she mutters, "Again? How many times are they going to start over?" She puts the files back and looks at me. "I'm Janice and I'll be your nurse today."

"What do you mean start over?"

A spark goes off in my head; tabula rasa is Latin for blank slate.

She waves a dismissive hand my way. "You'll have to talk to the doctor. Lucky for you, we're headed there right now."

Janice opens my door and an orderly brings in a wheelchair. Together they lift me from the bed and put me into the chair. We pass dozens of numbered doors identical to mine, each has a short inset window. When we reach an office door, she leaves me sitting outside next to an overstuffed leather sofa.

A gaunt man with large horn rimmed glasses steps out and greets me enthusiastically, "Rachel! How are you feeling today?"

He seems genuine, I have no cause to be rude. His oily red hair is unkempt and in need of a trim. Harvey Morris, M.D. is stitched on his rumpled lab coat .

"Fine, I suppose. Sore, my head's throbbing and I can't remember anything," I admit.

His pleased look dissolves. He takes off his glasses to polish them on his sleeve and responds, "Hmm...that must be bothersome." The words sound guilty.

Is he joking? Having no memory is a bit more than bothersome.

"The nurse mentioned something about starting over? She said I should talk to you about it. Does it have anything to do with the tabula rasa in my medical chart? What's Arcana?" The questions bubble out of me.

He averts his eyes. "I really couldn't say. Your chart was left in your room? I'll have to speak to the nurse. There's no need to cause you undue stress from reading a bunch of over inflated doctor's notes."

This is getting weirder by the second. What are they hiding from me?

My eyes dart nervously around "Could you tell me where I am?"

"You're at The Richland Institute," Morris offers. "The Richland Institute is a research and education center created to encourage select individuals to cultivate their latent potential and further the evolution of the human race." This speech sounds scripted.

Evolution? Like monkeys and Darwin?

Exasperated, I ask, "What could I possibly do to serve evolution?"

"We all perform our part," he answers cryptically.

That's a bullshit answer. Gonna need more info than that, buddy.

"Then tell me this good doctor, why does my part necessitate bars on my windows and a bolted door?" Hostility creeps into my voice. Clutching the arms on the wheelchair, I can feel myself starting to boil over.

God grant me the strength not to yell.

Glass rattles quietly, Dr. Morris apprehensively shifts from one foot to the other worrying his hands together behind his back. "Miss Ryan you don't need to get agitated. Today is a very busy day. We must hasten, or we'll be late."

Screw that! I'm not going anywhere with him.

"I want to go home. Who do I need to talk to so I can leave?"

Where is home? I don't know if I even have a place to go to, but I don't feel safe here.

"I don't think that's possible."

"I don't care! I want out of here now!" I feel myself begin to panic.

A picture frame flies off the wall and smashes onto the floor. Morris uses my distraction from the broken glass to commandeer my wheelchair.

"I promise, I'll speak to Mr. Richland on your behalf."

I want to get up and walk out, but I can't. My legs are weak. *What did they do to me?* It's like they stripped me of my free will to make my own choices. My fingers nervously pull at the gown to cover my thighs.

As Morris turns me around, he quickly heads to the elevator. We get out on the sixth floor and stop outside a steel door. *A bank vault?* Guards stand sentry on either side, strapped with some big ass guns.

Those guns look like they pack a serious punch. Note to self, don't get shot.

Doctor Morris flashes a security badge and a guard punches in a string of numbers on a console. The keypad chirps and the door opens. With an ominous moan, it hefts its own weight swinging outward. Inside is a tiled chamber similar to the ones in my room, but these are rusty brown instead of a snowy white. Dr. Morris helps me out of the wheelchair and stepping over the large mouth of the door, he leaves me. I jump as the behemoth door seals with a bang. I hear gears pushing locks into place. I put a hand against the wall to steady myself.

Crouched in the corner is a man. He has an average build, tawny skin and a mane of dark hair. If I had to guess, I would say he's South American.

It startles me when he looks at me and cries, "No, not again!"

He begins to rock back and forth twisting on his hair.

What the hell is wrong with him? Why is he freaking out? Is he afraid of me?

Too many questions, I have to get answers.

"Sir, do you know me?" I ask.

I take a few steps towards him, which sends him into a panic. He looks about ready to climb the walls. *Oo-kay. Never mind.* I can take a hint. He doesn't want me anywhere near him.

I retreat to the opposite side of the room. Putting my back to the wall, I slide down to sit. There are drains on the floor and sprinklers overhead. A window takes up a good portion of one wall, from the ceiling to about waist high. Men dressed in expensive suits assemble on the opposite side.

Are they here to watch me shower? Perverts.

A voice shatters my thoughts. I look back at the voyeurs. The speaker is an elderly man, with grayish hair cropped fashionably close to his head. A charming smile plays across his lips, his voice is smooth, but there is something about it that makes my skin crawl.

"Rachel meet Alonzo," he points to the man trembling in the corner. "Dr. Morris informs me you misplaced your memory again." The old man's cronies all chuckle like he told an amusing joke. "My name is Stuart Richland, we call this the testing tank. Here is where we analyze the truth of the phrase 'survival of the fittest'. Does brawn beat brains? Is the lion truly mightier than the lamb? We want to test survival abilities. It is unfortunate that only one of you will live, but many have died in the pursuit of scientific discovery. You should consider it an honor."

I struggle to my feet and cast myself at the viewing window. "Are you nuts?! Get me out of here! You can't do this to me it's illegal. It has to be!"

I can tell I'm getting nowhere; my pleas are simply a waste of energy. The men talk amongst themselves ignoring me. Mr. Richland crosses his arms over his chest. "The test will begin in five minutes. I advise you to gain your composure."

What's going on? Gain my composure, did he really just say to 'gain my composure'? What the hell have I gotten myself into?

I glance over at Alonzo. He's praying.

What were we supposed to do? Beat one another to death?

There is no way I can beat a grown man to death all by myself. I'm five-foot seven and could stand to lose a little weight, but there is no way I'm going to win a fistfight against a man. Banging on the glass I slide down on my knees.

"Let me out! What am I supposed to do? He's going to kill me! Please…"

Tapping the side of his head with his index finger Richland replies, "Everything you need is in here."

Smug son of a bitch. Shit. Can I kill someone, even to save my life?

My gaze drifts back to my rival. Alonzo is bent over on his hands and knees weeping. He sobs over and over saying something in a strange language.

I rub my eyes. For some reason Alonzo looks blurry. My eyes must be playing tricks on me, there is an immense form suspended above him. No, the form is a part of him; like an aura wavering out of sync. I blink several times to dismiss the phantom from my vision. Doesn't help. Alonzo gapes at me with fearful eyes, but the shape that rises out of him is eager. My mind tries to reconcile the insanity going on around me.

A computerized voice announces, "Testing commences now."

Alonzo wails. He contorts his body backward in an unnatural position that has him arching off the floor. His hands grab the shirt covering his chest as he forcibly rips it from his body. Fingernails rake down his ribs to his stomach taking bands of skin with them. They tear off in ribbons. Bones move under muscle as his nose and mouth elongate, shaping into a muzzle. Rolling over onto his belly, Alonzo's eyes reach mine. The pupils have changed to a burning yellow. Sharp teeth split his lips. Black fur sprouts out from between the mauled tissue.

I think I'm gonna puke.

In a blur, Alonzo springs into motion. His fist catches the

right side of my jaw. The force takes me off my feet and drives me back into the wall. Tiles come free from the impact. A copper tang fills my mouth. I spit and watch the crimson stain spread across the floor. Now I know what discolored the tile. Old blood and lots of it, soaked in to the ceramic and grout.

Slumped over against the wall I observe Alonzo in awe as he melts away and the phantom emanation takes over. I want to look away, but I can't. I'm looking at a werewolf. There is an awful sound bouncing off the walls, it takes me a minute to realize it's coming out of my mouth and I can't seem to stop the sound. Alonzo was medium in both size and stature, but the werewolf is tremendous. Somehow I manage to scramble out of the way before he can descend upon me again. I stand and stare at him. The wolf is enjoying himself. He has been let out of his cage and now he intends to have a little fun. Alonzo has assumed his place as the aura. He's quiet. The wolf will shield him.

What am I supposed to do? How am I expected to win? I must control my fear and find some advantage over this creature before me. I attempt to separate the man and beast. If I can see him as vulnerable, then I'll fear him less. After all, furry or not, it is still Alonzo.

Remember the man who was so scared of you that he cried, Rachel.

Shuddering he drops to one knee. Alonzo and the wolf are stretching apart. The beast is breaking off in one direction, Alonzo the opposite. It looks painful for them, but at the moment I don't much care.

Hurts huh? Good. Payback is a bitch named Rachel.

I put my hands out in front of me and imagine I'm rending seams. Howls and screeches fill the air. Flesh, muscle, and bone crack and tear. The two beings fall away from each other. I pulled Alonzo's wolf half into a corporeal being. I can't explain how, this shouldn't be possible. Blood is spattered on the walls and coats the floor. My hair is matted to my face with tears and blood.

I can't help but find some satisfaction in watching my aggressor come undone. The wolf dies immediately. It needed Alonzo more than Alonzo needed it. A parasite. The weakening man lays at my feet. I'm surprised at the gratitude in his eyes. How many times did he kill his challenger? How many lives has he been required to take to assure his own survival? By my hand, his wretched existence is done, and he's grateful.

Icy water cascades over me. Numb, I observe the blood fade to pink and escape down the drain. Violent shivers shake my body. I think I may be in shock.

The vault door reopens, and two men in hazmat suits come in with a body bag. They put both the wolf and man inside. Together they drag the heavy burden from the room. Another person in hazmat gear advances towards me—Janice. I back away. In her hands, she holds a scrub brush and soap. After harshly removing my hospital gown, she takes the soap and brush and scrubs me with vigor. She looks disgusted; I feel disgusted. Considering where she's employed, I want to ask her who the real monster is. You can't scour blood off of people while bodies are carted away and maintain your humanity. I glower at her until she averts her eyes.

Heartless bitch.

Buck naked in front of an audience is not my idea of fun.

God, this is so embarrassing.

A clump of Alonzo washes off me; bile rises in my throat. Janice jumps back as I vomit. When I stop heaving, I take stock of my body and find more pieces of Alonzo. Flesh and hair. *What the fuck! I've got werewolf in my hair! Get it off! Get it off!* I wrench the scrub brush out of Janice's hand and scour my body. When I am finished, my skin has angry red marks from where I rubbed it raw.

I'll never feel clean again.

Once I'm freshly dressed in a new hospital gown, they take me to a boardroom. Its walls are lined with expensive paintings. An elongated glass table is in the center of the room ringed by oversized black leather chairs. Richland convenes at the head of the table. As my chair is wheeled inside, the Armani squad, as I nicknamed them, stand up and clap. I'm speechless; did I not just commit murder?

Richland gets up last and says, "Well done Rachel! Quite the performance today."

I can't restrain my outrage, "Screw you, asshole!"

The gentleman on Richland's right frowns at me. "Apologize to Mr. Richland," he barks out angrily.

A calendar hangs on the wall, the kind you tear off the page every day to reveal the new date. Today is June 27, 2011.

I've been here over a year.

Hysterical laughter bubbles up out of me. This whole thing is absurd. Surely, I will wake up any moment. Dr. Morris looks at me concerned. My laughter turns to tears as overwhelming defeat settles in.

"It's alright, Mr. Gates." He smiles at me indulgently, "She's over excited. Since you're still suffering memory loss, I'll give you a swift education. Mr. Lopez was a werewolf. There are countless like him. At this time, we're uncertain how many species of preternatural beings exist. Vampires, werewolves, exotic cats, even dragons have been witnessed. Creatures you believed only lived in your nightmares are living among us. They lurk in plain sight. We chose you to help us bring down the demons. The doctors injected you with a virus to augment your natural psychic gift. On scans, your brain shows improvements, but until today you had yet to manifest anything transmundane. What you achieved today was made possible by the introduction of a patented pharmaceutical called Arcana. With science and psychic sensitives like yourself, we have created a way to fight all that's corrupt within the world."

His long-winded lecture gives me a headache. I rub at the cutting pain behind my eyes and wearily ask, "Ripping men apart with my mind, is that the extent of what I can expect from Arcana?"

I must have lost it. I'm talking like this is a normal, an everyday occurrence. After you've dismembered a werewolf with your mind not much surprises you, I guess.

Richland has no answers to give, but Dr. Morris is more forthcoming. "I'm not certain if we've seen all you can do. By nature, the virus is always mutating. You may never reach full potential, or you could've already topped out."

They turned me into a monster. Tears are rolling down my face, but I don't make a sound. Dr. Morris looks away, and I refuse to make eye contact with anyone else. I hate that they made me cry.

Please, let me wake up.

"Perhaps Miss Ryan should rest now," Dr. Morris interjects softly.

I don't want to rest because I am already asleep. This can't be real.

An orderly takes charge of the wheelchair. Down the hallway to my room we pass the same doors as before, but this time I see people looking out from the windows. Every face conveys a story; fear and anxiety for their future, curiosity for who I am, and defeat.

How long do you live like this before you accept it?

In my room, which is really a cell, a tray is resting on my bed with a ham sandwich, bottled water, and a shiny red apple. My stomach growls with hunger.

Can you be hungry in a dream? Who am I kidding, this is no dream. It's a waking nightmare.

At least I'll get some food in my stomach before I sleep. The food is tasteless, but I devour every bite. Once my stomach is full, and I set the tray down on the floor, I crawl under the covers. In sleep, I pray I can forget again. In my dreams, I hope I'll be free.

If this is the real world, my dreams have to be better.

Futile thoughts. If I can sleep at all, I'll replay all the horror I've been a party to.

CHAPTER 2

July 1

Winter

THE HUMAN REALM used to be the safer place compared to my home in Fairy. That was before *something* started preying on the preternatural. I hitch the strap of my bag higher on my shoulder, checking it's still secure. There's a decent sized blade in it along with several hidden on my body. You don't live long in the Fae Court if you can't defend yourself. Give me a sword and I'm really good, but give me knives and I'm the best. I haven't had much cause to use them during my time pretending I'm human. Practicing with the Wraiths keeps me sharp.

Never thought I'd be sparing with the elite vampire secret service.

I fell into the arrangement with the Wraiths by accident. A hyena therian tried to grab me over the top of the bar at the Lune Rouge where I work. He was drunk off his ass and not taking no of any kind for an answer. I punctuated my disinterest in his advances with a carefully placed knife to the ribs. My boss, Claude Bonvillian, and his son Bastien made sure he knew he wasn't welcome back ever again.

Nikolai Domitru was in the Lune Rouge that night. Of

course no one knew he was there, that's why he leads the Wraiths. No one does hidden as well as Nikolai.

I swear he could hide in the desert dressed in black at high noon.

The vampire scared me when he appeared on my apartment doorstep. Vamps didn't exactly look fondly on the Fae.

Who does?

"Relax," he'd said. "I wanted to offer you a job, if I wanted to kill you, you'd be dead already."

I swallowed and laughed nervously, "Heh. Uh yeah. If you wanted me dead I doubt you'd knock on the door."

"I might." He shrugged. "Personally, I prefer the fight over a quick kill. It's more sporting that way."

"Not helping me feel safe," I muttered. "So what's the job? I already work at Lune Rouge full time."

Nikolai waved off my concern. "We can work around your schedule. The way you moved with a blade was impressive. I can use a knife but I can't wield it like a natural extension of my body. Do you think you could teach someone how to do it?"

"Uhh, yeah, sure." Am I nuts for agreeing? "You want me to teach you?"

He shook his head, "I want you to teach all of the men and women in the ranks of the Wraith."

From that moment on I became the Wraith's Blademaster. I'm proud of my students, but I still like to keep a safe distance when we aren't training. You never know when a vampire is going to get a wild hair and dispose of another Fae.

You might ask me why I'm nervous walking home at three

o'clock in the morning if I'm such a badass. The answer is, much deadlier people than me have disappeared or been found dead within the past year.

Pride goeth before a fall.

I take all the precautions I can to ensure my survival, especially when I don't know who is the enemy. Weapons? Check! Fastest and most well lit route home? Check! Phone call to check in with my best friend Tsura as soon as I hit the door? Check, or she shows up at my house very unhappy.

Okay, I lied. I don't avoid all vampires.

Tsura Tymar is a vampire and she's one of two people I'd trust with my life. Madalaina Bonvillian is the other person, she's a wolf therian. I met Madalaina working for her dad and she introduced me to Tsura. Our species don't play nice in closed quarters historically, but we make it work. We bonded over our mommy issues. Madalaina's mom is also a mentally unbalanced raging bitch. Tsura never knew her mom. She was murdered for being the human wife of a vampire a super long time ago.

Speaking of people gone for a long time....

Madalaina's has two older brothers; Athan was born first followed by Bastien. Athan disappeared years before I arrived. He was one of the first people to go missing. Now there's a wall in the back of the Lune Rouge papered with flyers several inches deep. They all say the same thing, have you seen me? The pictures of the lost are haunting because you know you might be next.

The blinding lights of The Richland Institute shine in front of me. If this weren't the quickest way home I'd avoid it to stay away from that place alone. It looks benign but I feel something sinister lives there. The lights shine too bright, like they're trying to prove they have nothing to hide. I keep my head down and hurry past. Getting home in one piece is all I care about. Making waves attracts attention and that's the last thing I need.

CHAPTER 3

July 2

Rachel

SEVERAL DAYS PASS UNEVENTFULLY. Someone brings me food three times a day and I'm allowed to use the bathroom after each meal. Every other day I can shower if I choose. They can hold me prisoner and force me to fight for my life but letting me go longer than a day without a bath must be what they consider cruel and unusual punishment. The rest of my day is spent staring at the walls of my room. I take the time to wrap my head around the existence of the wolf man. I make the conscious decision to accept what Richland told me. I could freak out, but what purpose would it serve? Yes, the supernatural is real. I've seen it.

Can't deny a werewolf when it is beating the crap out of you.

Sleep is elusive. When it occurs, I dream of monsters and death. There is a nagging feeling in the back of my mind that I already knew this. Deja vu plagues me.

Why does it feel like I've been through this song and dance before?

The familiarity of the situation irritates me. Like so many other memories, I can't quite grasp them out of the ether.

Amnesia is a pain in the ass.

Some memories are resurfacing en masse. I remember I was a sophomore at a community college studying Journalism. Tuition was high and I had several student loans. I used to live in a rattrap apartment, in the poor part of town, within walking distance of the gas station I worked at. The wages suck, but it covered rent. I was busy with classes, work, and studying. Until I met Anna, I had no friends. Anna is smart and beautiful; I envy her. She came into the shop one night to buy a candy bar. My schoolbooks were laying on the counter, she asked about my major and where I went to school. We talked for almost an hour before she had to leave. The next night she came back. We were best friends from then on. Anna persuaded me to move out of my crappy apartment. She needed a roommate, and I wanted to live someplace safer.

"That area is a murder scene waiting to happen. At least hookers don't hang out on the corner of my building," Anna told me.

Anna brought home a project from her psychology professor. The subject was the brain, and what laid locked within. Mostly, it was just a mess of vague questions and absurd riddles. I didn't comprehend what the test actually determined, but took it anyway since Anna asked. I believed in the subject of the test. Psychics and the capacity to do things others can't.

I never told Anna about my dreams, the ones about events that haven't happened yet. I get impressions of people and places. I've only told one soul, my best friend, when I was eleven.

I grew up in a small town in the heart of the Bible Belt.

Religion was the cornerstone of the community.

Too bad we had a nutcase for a pastor.

Brother George was a fire and brimstone preacher. Convinced the Devil hid in every shadow bent on destroying us. Television was the devil. Modern music was the devil. A woman who didn't submit to her husband's every whim was possessed by the Devil. I should have known better than to say anything about my gift, but I was a kid. I warned my friend Alice about her ill grandmother but she didn't believe me. When her grandmother died suddenly, she told her parents and they blamed me. Brother George claimed I was a witch.

If I were really a witch, I would have made it rain candy.

My parents elected to move and I hid my ability after that.

Two months after the test I received a letter from the private university Anna attended. An invitation to join a special study. I was skeptical at first, but I knew I couldn't pass up the opportunity. The university agreed to transfer all of the credits I had previously earned and apply them to my degree. They paid off my student loans at the community college and provided me with a scholarship that would pay for everything. I didn't ask questions because I was afraid they might realize they had made a mistake. The study required me to take many aptitude tests each week, and then I was able to attend all my regular classes.

The last memory I have before I woke up in this place was coming home to an empty apartment and finding Anna, along with all of her stuff, had disappeared. Upon closer investigation of the emptied apartment, I discovered a stranger in her bedroom. The intruder didn't give me time to react as he swiftly jumped me, and forced me face down on the carpet. I felt a stinging sensation on the side of my neck, and the world began to blur at the fringes of my vision.

Agent Acquisition. Was it the stranger in our apartment or Anna?

I hope Anna is okay, but it's all too coincidental. Her friendship, the study, and the generous offer from the college. My mind and memories line up the events as the fear in my gut bubbles over. This was a set-up from day one.

Why expend all that energy and time on me?

Janice checks my vital signs daily, but no doctors harass me for almost a week. The days and nights drag without incident. I've been bored out of my mind until today. To pass the time, I've been flexing my Arcana. Nothing big. Just a light show for my own amusement. The first two things that happened terrified me. I set my pillow on fire twice and zapped the hell out of myself a dozen times. I did pick up a few new tricks like astral projection; in a way I was able to 'walk' around the Institute.

Occasionally, I connected with one or two of the other inmates. I tapped into their fear and pain, but anger became the most common factor between us all. While I was 'visiting' my neighbors, I tried to soothe them. Help them find a moment of peace; let them know they aren't alone. I stopped messing around with my outreach program when I encountered *him*. Cold controlled rage. He frightened me. Whoever he is, he has plans.

This afternoon Janice showed me the library. I nearly

hugged her. I suspect Richland isn't comfortable having a disgruntled psychic sitting around with too much free time. Does he think a field trip to the library is going to earn him brownie points?

Golly gee, thanks Mr. Richland! This totally makes up for turning me into a mutant.

An African American man is seated at a desk playing a game of chess. *Another inmate like me?* Desperate for the social interaction I walk over and introduce myself.

Without glancing up, he nods, "Hello, child. I'm Kadema Sidell. Call me Papa Sidell. The rest of my congregation does." He motions for me to take the chair across from him. "How does this day find you?" He's stiff and formal. It strikes me as funny considering we're both prisoners.

Dude, lighten up.

I've been sitting in a room for days. Sitting isn't high on my agenda, but I don't want to annoy my potential new friend. I take my place and answer him, "I guess I can't complain. I mean I haven't been attacked by any werewolves lately."

He grins at me, "Yes, I think that could be viewed as progress."

His unguarded king is wide open on the board. I could end the game with one move. A piece shoots across and takes out the king, sending it flying off the table. Telekinesis.

Jiminy Cricket! That's new. Watch it, Rachel. Don't tip your hand to the other players. It gives them an advantage over you.

"Do you mind if I ask you a question, Kadema?"

He looks up from resetting the chess pieces to study me, "Anyone can ask anything child, but whether they get an answer is uncertain."

Great, more riddles. I just adore riddles.

"I killed a man in the tank. How do I live with that?"

I wait for his reaction. His face never changes. No loathing or shock. He considers me a moment before asking, "Do you believe you did wrong?"

I fidget in the chair a little. "At first I was ashamed of myself, but he would have killed me if I hadn't gotten him first. At this point I'm just happy to be alive."

Though, it'd be nice if my living arrangements improved.

Kadema shrugs "You were not the assassin, but the instrument. The puppeteer lays behind a wall of glass. We're weaponry in a war. But that was not the questions you wanted answered, was it?"

I try to think how to word it but can't so I blurt out, "How did he become a werewolf? Was he born that way?"

Kadema shakes his head no, "Some are born, others are made. The ones who are born don't share a body with the beast and have proven harder for Richland to catch. They are the beasts. It's much more difficult to catch a predator who has been hunting its whole life."

"The made ones, how are they made?"

"Only born shifters can create others," he explained, "either by birth or bite. The bitten are sterile."

Janice hovers in the doorway.

Recess must be over.

I stand up to go. Kadema startles me by clutching my fingers.

"Why will you not call me Papa Sidell like the others? I could be a savior to you in this place, child." Magical vibrations leap off Kadema's skin and up my arm. This man has enough power to level the whole building.

This isn't like my arcana, he was born this way. I can sense the difference between his magic and my own. Manufactured versus born magic. His grip is too tight to pull away.

"You said your congregation calls you that, well I won't worship you." The words come out sharp. I tug again to free my hand but nothing. My pulse quickens. "You're no savior of mine."

A satisfied sneer spreads across his face. "You fear me."

The uptight SOB is feeding off my fear. What an asshole!

I feel his magic trying to read me in some way. Now I'm pissed off. "I'm not stupid, of course I fear you. I feared the wolf too and I tore him apart easy as a sheet of paper."

I kind of sound psycho but damn it I am mad.

If Kadema wants to play a power game, I'll play. I push back at him using what I've learned on my own. Blue sparks zip down my arm and up Kadema's. His eyes glow electric blue. A vision hits me.

I'm standing in Kadema's village; legions of followers come from all over to solicit his services. A small boy, his son, is playing in the yard next to the house. Kadema's glory and arrogance angers his rivals. So the child is murdered to humble Kadema. The ploy backfires when Kadema forces the dead out of their graves. He sets them upon the other villages on the island. His army of corpses tear every man, woman, and child limb from limb. The ocean around the island runs red from all the blood. Kadema is not satisfied until he is the last living human left standing.

Kadema hisses and releases me, "You see things I won't allow."

Damn skippy.

"I want nothing to do with what's in your head," I bite out. "You try that shit on me ever again and I'll find out how far my power will let me dig in there."

The ever-present guards watch tensely. None of them bold enough to step between us. Janice moves forward in their place. "Alright you two, let's break it up."

Guess she's the only one with balls big enough to risk her neck. Does that make her brave or stupid?

Kadema laughs at her and turns his attention to the chess game once again.

Stupid. Definitely stupid.

* * *

The next morning an orderly comes to get me for another round of testing in the tank. I scowl at him.

You're not supposed to shoot the messenger, but a little maiming would be okay, right?

All the usual suspects are present: Richland, Dr. Morris, Armani squad, and armed sentries. A beautiful Japanese woman is pacing the length of the tank. She notices me and gives a slight nod in my direction.

She isn't screaming. Step in the right direction from last time.

Richland clears his throat to get our attention. "Rachel I want you to meet Taka. You both know how this test ends. You may begin at your leisure." He takes his seat.

I look over at Taka. Her eyes are reptilian now.

Is she a lizard?

Not a lizard, a dragon.

Just peachy.

I don't know if I can haul something that big apart. Taka doesn't move, she isn't in a hurry to attack. Maybe we're on the same page about this. I choose to take a chance.

"I don't want to hurt you and I don't think you want to hurt me. They can't make us do anything can they?"

Taka shrugs and takes a place on the tile floor. I follow suit on the opposite side of the room. We don't move for minutes; Richland begins pacing behind the glass.

"Well ladies, someone needs to do something." I can tell he is getting angry by the edge to his voice.

"Pass. I think we'll just sit here and get to know each other better," I return. "Got a deck of cards we could borrow?"

Taka laughs. I shouldn't poke the angry bear, but damn I have to get my kicks somewhere.

Richland is becoming purple. He's definitely angry. "I'm afraid not, ladies. Open the door, put the girl in." The vault door opens; a little girl is pushed in.

"If neither you nor Miss Fujiwara will comply then the child will be eliminated." Richland sneers at us. Dr. Morris is trying to protest, but Richland won't hear it.

"You're a bastard!" I yell at him. Taka doesn't look mad, but grimly thoughtful instead.

Our obvious distress has its desired effect. Richland takes his chair again. "You only have a few minutes to settle her fate."

The girl wraps her arms around her middle and cries. She can't be older than five. My chest constricts with a fierce need to protect her. Taka walks over and kneels down in front of her. Frightened, the child tries to move away from the stranger before her, but Taka holds her in place by her forearms.

"It is okay little one." Taka motions at me to come closer.

She sniffles, "My name is Livia."

I pick her up in my arms. "Hello, Livia. My name is Rachel, and this is Taka." Livia lays her head on my shoulder and cries silently. In my arms, I feel something strange emanating from within her.

I don't exactly have the time to investigate that now. She's not a regular little girl though.

Taka strokes her back to soothe her. "You don't need to be afraid, Livia. Rachel is going to keep you safe."

"What are you doing?" I whisper.

"I'm weary" she sighs. "I don't have the will to face this place any longer."

Eyeing her suspiciously, I urge, "What are you planning to do?"

A brilliant smile graces her lips. The light doesn't touch her eyes. "Please don't allow the child to watch. I don't want her to have nightmares."

After a fierce hug for us both, Taka approaches the viewing glass. "Richland, you crave blood and death. Fine. I'll give it to you."

Taka's nails curve into talons. I press Livia's head against my shoulder to prevent her from looking up. Guards are working to unlock the door. They fumble into the vault. I shrink back with Livia in hopes of escaping any reprisal. When the guards are within arm's reach of Taka, she lets her hand fly to her throat. Violent slashes run downward, the motion tears clumps of flesh out, blood spurts across the glass.

Oh my god! There's so much.

Dr. Morris and the Armani squad sit frozen. Taka's body crumbles to the floor. Richland is incensed. I find myself weeping with Livia.

Richland pounds the window with his fist, "You think you won! You only demonstrated how far you would go to protect that child."

I am afraid to use Arcana with Livia in my arms.

What if it hurts her?

Guards jerk Livia away from me. She screeches for me. My Arcana is rising. Blue flashes ricochet off the tiles. I can't harness it in time to stop another guard from using the butt of his gun to knock me out.

CHAPTER 4

July 4

Winter

THE AIR FEELS UNEASY. If I had to describe it I'd say it's like I'm standing on the precipice of great change. We all know change isn't easy. The kind of change that blankets every living creature and sends a stir through the universe. It's already happened, I just haven't seen it yet. Every rock thrown into the water causes a ripple. One of the ripples was growing closer to me and I was helpless to prevent it.

I stood behind the bar and surveyed the crowd gathered for the Fourth of July party. Claude was home with his wife Adele and his son and daughter were in attendance. Bastien leaned against a table chatting up a random girl I wasn't familiar with. Madalaina sat in front of me sipping on a club soda. She waved a hand in my face.

"Earth to Winter!" She laughed at my startled expression.

"Sorry, Madalaina. I'm spacing tonight."

"I noticed," she grinned.

A bottle blonde, she is the most unique among the Bonvillian clan. Her pale blonde hair against her family's dark features wasn't the only difference. Her father, Claude, is a businessman and the Alpha Prime on the Therian Council.

That means he's the top guy in their world. All the shape-shifters in Ardmore had their own alpha to listen too in addition to Claude as the Alpha Prime. Adele Bonvillian is a notorious ice queen without a heart. I don't think Adele likes anyone, maybe not even her own mate.

Poor Claude.

Handsome and charming, Bastien, could take his pick of bed partners without fear of refusal. He had a way of making any woman feel like the only one alive when he talked to her. This might've caused some problems around here, but it was common knowledge Bastien didn't have the word 'commitment' in his vocabulary. He fills in as a manager at the Lune Rouge from time to time so I know him fairly well. As well as you can know a man guarding his secrets behind a façade of assured control.

Madalaina is the most open hearted, friendly creature I've ever met. I wonder what it's like to live without enemies. I can't see how Madalaina could have any. Fun, outgoing, pretty but not vain, and loyal; Madalaina is one of the few friends that I have. She's a bit of a party girl but it's all for show. Adele wants Madalaina under her thumb so she rebels by spending her every waking moment out, frequently at the Lune Rouge with me or visiting Tsura in her home.

Some party girl. Ha! Her choices are the establishment owned by her dad or the only other vampire guarded as closely as The Regis, their king.

She looked over her shoulder at Bastien and shouted, "Hey! Are you done flirting yet? I'd like to play pool sometime before I'm old and grey."

Bastien ignored his little sister but the object holding his interest turned bright red. She scooted around Bastien and made a hasty exit from the building. After rolling his eyes heaven ward and mumbling something to himself, he joined Madalaina and I at the bar.

"Cock blocked by my own sister." He tries to sound wounded but an impish grin breaks through.

Madalaina smacks his shoulder with the back of her hand. "Whatever, we're here to play pool. You have enough groupies, no need to add more to your harem."

I laugh at their exchange.

"Hey Winter, how's it going tonight?" Bastien asks.

"It's going, boss man." My voice is overly cheerful to divert his shrewd assessment. I don't want to talk about my worries.

Bastien watches me, considering whether to push the issue with me or not. He can tell I'm not being up front with him.

After draining the last of her drink Madalaina hops off the barstool. "Leave her alone and let's go already."

To my relief Bastien relents. I mouth a thank you to my friend once his back his turned. She winks at me as she heads up to the loft where the pool tables are. I do my best to shake off my anxiety and focus on my work.

CHAPTER 5

July 4

Rachel

WAKING UP IN FOREIGN PLACES *is becoming a habit of mine. This time I am in a limousine. At least I get to ride in style.*

Someone changed me from the hospital gown to street clothes. I shudder at the thought of anyone from Richland having access to my naked body while knocked out. I run my hands over the mint green polo tracing the little hot pink jockey symbol over my left breast. Light colored khaki pants and brown loafers complete the country club chic ensemble.

This outfit needs to be burned.

There is a throbbing above my right eyebrow where the guard in the tank hit me. Livia is sleeping on the seat next to me with her head resting in my lap. She looks peaceful and angelic, wild red hair in disarray. Richland's right-hand man, Gates, is seated across from me.

He's the guy who demanded I apologize to Richland on the first day.

He has a medicine container in one hand and a bottle of water in the other.

"Would you like an aspirin?" He asks.

I am hesitant to take them. In the end, my head hurts too much for me to be picky about where the relief comes from. I pop the top off the aspirin bottle and wash a pill down with a swig of water.

He narrows his eyes at my injury and says, "The guard left a nasty cut, but it looks like you are healing fast."

I gingerly touch the area, it's still sore but I can't feel the cut so I peel the sticky tape off.

"Where are we headed?"

He straightens his tie casually. "We're on our way to the Lune Rouge."

That's odd. Are we going dancing?

"The night club, over on Main and Sixth?"

"Oui. The name means 'red moon' in French. The club has been owned and operated by shape-shifters for twenty years. The current proprietor is a werewolf named Claude Bonvillian. Our insider reports are mostly shifters, but the occasional vampire wanders in; although it's not encouraged. The ordinary people who frequent Lune Rogue are clueless they're mixing with animals." Repugnance twists his features. "All non-humans need to be destroyed. They're demons, unnatural in our world. You will help us purge them from the Earth. You should be thanking Richland for this opportunity!"

Woo! Someone needs to up his dosage.

Gates' yelling rouses Livia. She sits up and rubs the sleep from her eyes. "Where are we going?" She mumbles.

I don't want to scare her, so I try for cheerful enthusiasm. "We're going on a field trip. Won't that be fun?" She looks at me as if I'm an idiot.

Yeah, it does sound stupid. Sorry, kiddo.

I wrap an arm around her shoulders and pull her closer. The visor that separates the driver from us comes down. We've almost reached our destination. Butterflies form in my stomach. This is not a social call. They want me to do something terrible.

"My neck hurts." Livia whines. I move her hair out of the way to examine the spot. A wide blister has formed around a puncture wound. The skin is purple, radiating out into a sickly green. I touch the injury gently with the pad of my finger. Clear fluid dribbles out.

"What did you do, Gates?"

They don't care who they hurt, not even a child.

Gates smirks. "Insurance to guarantee your cooperation. It's apparent that Livia is our only leverage over you. Do you want to know the reason for your amnesia? We couldn't figure out how to break you, every time you became too much to handle we just started over. Erased you to a more manageable state. Imagine the damage it did?"

In the Institute, the nurse said they started over again. She meant they erased my memory. Again, she said. tabula rasa. How many times did they reset me?

Gates and his employer had hijacked my life.

"Why are you telling me this?" I demanded.

Gates shrugs. "We can reset you again if we have any problems. Somehow I think knowing will make you more agreeable not less."

He's right. I don't want to start again. I will find a way out of this, for Livia. First things first, I need to know what they did to her.

Stroking the soft hair on Livia's head I ask, "Will she be okay? What did they give her?"

Gates is peering out the window, bored with our discussion. "Another virus. Not Arcana, an older formula that didn't perform within accepted parameters. Don't fret, we made an antidote as well." He examines his nails, barely paying attention to me.

And if I believe that, you have a bridge to sell me in London.

My gut tells me he's lying about a cure. "So unless I do what you want, Livia will die?" I clarify.

"Correct. The process is quite painful." The way he looks at Livia makes my skin crawl. It's like he's excited to watch her suffer.

Sadistic bastard.

The limo rolls to a stop. Headlights beam in through the back window. A Humvee pulls up behind us. Gates gestures towards the door, "Ladies first."

Climbing out of the limousine, I am joined by Richland Institute guards from the Humvee.

"Cover the exits," Gates says over his shoulder.

Outside, I get my first close-up look of the club. Lune Rouge is a magnificent building. Not overly large, but with plenty of room for a small crowd. While it does not possess the pizzazz high end clubs do, it feels inviting. A subtle charm. The kind of place where everyone feels like a regular. The sign features a wolf under a large red moon with the club's name in big white letters.

Gates takes Livia's hand from me and holds it in his own. I hate that he is touching her. She didn't say a word in the limo as we talked about her fate.

So young, she doesn't understand what is going on.

I take the lead with Gates and Livia behind me. The five guards in civilian clothing bring up the rear. I don't see any weapons.

Must be concealed somewhere on their bodies. I highly doubt they're walking into a shifter club unarmed.

I push my way through the door and look the interior over. A bar is installed in the back right corner. There are three sets of booths and a scattering of tables on either side of the entrance. Straight back are the doors to the kitchen along with a staircase that leads upstairs to a loft. A few foosball tables and two arcade games fill out the first floor. Looks like a full house tonight. Probably a Fourth of July party. Shifters are everywhere.

Auras, auras, everywhere.

Just like with Alonzo in the tank, I can see the animal inside them.

I understand what Kadema meant about made versus born shifters now. The bitten have the displaced aura. A mirage that wavers over them. With born shifters, it's all in the eyes. They look inhuman for a split second. If I concentrate, I can hold it longer and even see the beast contort their face. Doing a quick count I find wolves, bears, and cats. Whatever Gates organized, we will fail. Too many of them against one of me. My heart sinks in my chest.

I can't win this.

Just inside the door Gates raises a gun from inside his suit and shoots into the ceiling. Initially the shifters look tense, but after realizing it's just a bunch of humans they visibly relax. Their expressions vary. Some are amused, others annoyed. Several shifters have gone back to whatever they were doing before Gates shot the gun. The music has been turned down; only a few people are talking quietly. Gates and his guards move deeper into Lune Rouge, guns drawn.

Why are they shifters letting them pass? They certainly don't appear to feel threatened.

Gates is in the center of the club. I follow behind him curious to see what happens next.

Up in the loft people are lined up against the railing watching the display below. My eyes are drawn to one man in particular. From my angle and with the low lighting, I can't tell much about his features or height. His clothes and hair are dark; he rests one arm on the top rail and holds a pool cue in the other hand. His gaze is a penetrating green, I swear his eyes glow, and I have to make myself look away.

I should grab Livia and run.

"Guns are not appreciated here, sir," says a slender young woman behind the bar. She cleans the bar top with a rag, barely giving us her attention.

Liquid courage, come to mama!

Moving around Gates, I walk over and take a seat in front of her. "Can I get a drink please?" I ask politely.

"What do you think you are doing?" Gates grinds out through clenched teeth. He is standing directly behind me.

"You folks had me locked up playing lab rat for a year. I just want a few minutes of me time before the shit hits the fan."

Gates doesn't know what to say to that. Patrons watch me curiously. Let them. I am past the point of caring. The bartender grins at me. Silvery lavender hair dances around her shoulders. Her eyes are a mesmerizing shade of purple. She doesn't seem real. I am spellbound.

Not a shifter, what is she?

I have to stop myself from reaching out and touching her.

"What would you like?" She asks me breaking the trance.

Back to reality, in a room full of doom. "What would you recommend for a woman's last drink on Earth?"

Now I have everyone's attention. No one is talking anymore and someone turned off the music. The bartender is bothered. She chews on her bottom lip and frowns at me. I don't like knowing these people are scared of me.

I reach a hand across the bar in friendship. "Hi, I'm Rachel. Kidnap victim and shut in. The little lady behind me is Livia, she's the loud mouth's insurance policy to make me toe the line."

"Winter," she grins and shakes my hand. "Exiled Fae princess."

Gates is growing annoyed.

"What are you blathering on about, Miss Ryan?"

I'm ignoring him. The bartender thinks for a second and says, "For your last drink on Earth I'd suggest whiskey. The good stuff. Aged, single barrel." She pours a shot and hands it to me. Her hand touches mine and this time when our eyes lock a connection forms. Warmth and comfort course through me. When she disengages her hand from mine I'm disappointed. Once again, dread and fear take over.

Downing my shot, I shake it off. I've never had whiskey before. If I live, I won't repeat the experience. *Blech!*

"Rachel, I am talking to you!" Gates is losing what grip he has left on his temper.

Waving that gun around, he looks like a raving lunatic.

I am losing my temper too. Alcohol loosens my tongue. "Oh hold your damn horses. Are you really so eager to die?"

Stumped, Gates asks, "Why would *we* die?"

I huff. "I count a few different flavors of shifter in here and only six guns. I don't even know if a gun can kill a shape shifter." I turn and raise a brow at Winter.

"Depends," she shrugs. "You'd need a lot of complex ammunition to do 'em all. Then you'd still have the non-weres to deal with." She says matter-of-factly.

Peachy! I need an armory of special ammunition. Too bad I left that at home.

"We don't need special ammunition," Gates scoffs. "We have you, Rachel."

He's putting a lot of faith in my Arcana. "I killed one werewolf. One!" I stress the word. "I didn't even do it on purpose! What makes you think I can do a roomful all at once? You don't expect them to wait patiently in line do you?"

He cannot possibly be that stupid.

The whiskey is affecting me, I feel light headed. I grip the bar to calm the spinning. Gates looks baffled by my question then it dawns on me, "Aw geez, you do expect me to wipe them all out. You are a dangerously stupid man."

"And you are wasting Livia's time," he counters.

A guard grabs my upper arm and pulls me off the stool. A growl from nearby scares him and he lets me go. I stumble sideways to catch myself and look for the source of the sounds. The guy from the loft with the incredible green eyes snuck down when no one was looking.

My knight in shining armor.

He's down at the other end of the bar glaring daggers at Gates. Still not close enough to really check him out. I can see he's tall and well built, but right now I really need to pay attention to crazy Gates and his boys.

Gates is a lost cause. I plead with the guards closest to me. "I can promise you we won't survive this…One of them will snap my neck or Gates will give the order to execute me. Livia and I are dead in any scenario."

I'll give Richland credit for hiring dedicated guards. They don't even flinch.

Gun pointed at me, Gates rages, "Damn it! Why can't you do what you're supposed to?!"

I square off against him. "You're pushing the wrong person. I'm beyond the point of caring how badly I hurt you! Let Livia go, and I won't twist you up in knots."

For a moment, Gates blanches, but recovers quickly. "You think you can barter with me? Kill her now."

A guard reaches out to grab me.

"Don't touch me!" My voice is dangerously high. He soars backward, a support beam running from the floor to the loft above catches him in the back. His spine cracks like a twig. Gates gapes at me.

I shrug. "I warned you."

He retaliates by wrenching Livia's arm behind her back until it curves at an abnormal angle and I hear an audible snap. Livia screams. Using her body as a shield Gates edges towards the exit.

"Shut up!" Gates bellows and jerks her hard making her yelp louder.

Fire ignites under my skin. All I want now is to make Gates suffer. "That was a big mistake."

People are yelling all around me. The guards move closer together for protection. The shifters are no longer spectators. Growls and snarls fill the air. When Gates broke the child's arm he started a chain of events. Gunfire erupts as one shifter leaps to take a guard down.

Electric pulses build under my skin so fast I can't hold it. I fixate on Gates looking for vulnerabilities. Alonzo was a werewolf and Gates is just a run of the mill human. No shapes to divide from his body. Nothing that defines him as supernatural, giving me little to work with. My thumping heart echoes inside my head. Another heartbeat joins in. This one belongs to Gates and it is racing. I know it's his heart because it beats in time with the pulse jumping at his throat. He's terrified of what I'm going to do to him. I focus all my energy on his heart. I squeeze. Gates clutches at his chest, letting go of Livia in the process. He opens his mouth to yell, and a blue beam spills out of him.

Livia hits the floor, and a stout guy in a biker jacket scoops her up and out of the way. Gates staggers forward and crumples to his knees. Chaos erupts as the patrons of the Lune Rouge annihilate the remaining three of Richland's guards. Gates puts to use his remaining strength to raise the gun and fire it at me. The bullet catches my shoulder, and I fall. My skull bounces off the plank floor before settling.

Livia appears by my side. She strokes my hair with her good hand and pleads with me. "Rachel. Please, don't leave me."

Hot tears edge out the corner of my eye.

What will become of Livia? Who will take care of her?

The lavender haired bartender kneels down next to me and catches my hand. Her lips are moving, but I hear nothing. Darkness consumes me.

CHAPTER 6

July 4

Winter

I DIDN'T HAVE THE MAGIC to save a life. It was stripped from me when I was exiled. Holding one of the woman's hands in my own and applying pressure to her bullet wound with the other, I wait for help. The little girl is sobbing. Madalaina sits on her knees next to the child and tries in vain to soothe her. The harder she cries her magic becomes more and more unstable. It's dormant, and would've remained so longer if she hadn't been traumatized. Unlike the unconscious woman's manufactured magic, the child's is natural.

I search out one of the waitresses, a lioness named Daisy. From across the room I call to her. "Get Seraphina from next door!"

Daisy nods and runs. If you were to just walk past, the Witch's Brew appears to be a teashop, but it's a front for the real business. Seraphina is a powerful, natural born witch. She uses her skills to craft anything from air freshener to poison. Herbs from Secrets of the Sea would be better but we don't have the time for someone to go all the way to shore and back.

Seraphina bursts through the door and tosses a brown bag

onto the floor. It opens on impact and a spray of powder shoots into the air. Lyssa, a snake therian, has been corralling all the humans in the bar; with the entrance of Seraphina they all go still and quiet.

"Tell them whatever you want, they won't remember what they've seen," she says.

Hurrying to my side Seraphina removes my hand and slaps a wet cloth over the wound.

"Hold that on. It'll pull the bullet out and then we can wrap it."

"Is she gonna live?" Bastien is standing behind his sister, alternating between watching the woman and the child.

"She'll live," Seraphina confirmed.

"Ssshe sshouldn't," Lyssa hisses.

"Why not? She didn't hurt any of us?" Madalaina argues.

Bastien puts up a hand to shut them both down before they start yelling. "I already called dad. There's an emergency meeting at our home. Once the woman is stable I'm to bring her and the child there." Bastien pulls his shirt off and tosses it at his sister. "Wrap her arm, that bastard broke it."

"Have you looked at her, Bastien?" She stares at the girl in question with wide eyes. "She looks just like…"

"I know," he cuts her off, harshly. "Get it done, Madalaina."

"What's your name, sweetheart?" Carefully she uses Bastien's shirt as a sling for the broken arm.

Her crying has died down to a hiccupping sniffle. Exhausted from tears and pain, her eyes are droopy. "Livia," she answers.

I study the child next to the witch and the woman on the floor. Magic is tangible. For those who practice it without benefit of birth, it's artifice shows. For example the woman, Rachel they called her, her magic has a manufactured smell. My nose picks up on steel and ozone in the air. Seraphina's magic reminds me of wind before a thunderstorm. Livia's is all fresh air and flowers, there's a wildness to it. Something I haven't seen since I left Fairy behind me.

The magic, her hair; do they know what creature has landed in their lap?

I couldn't say who she reminded Bastien or Madalaina of, but I knew without a doubt who she was to me.

How did she get here?

The child suddenly slumps to the ground and her body begins to shake as a violent seizure overtakes her.

CHAPTER 7

July 5

Rachel

MORE THAN ONCE I tried to claw my way up from unconsciousness. I remain unable to move through the arguing and crying, people prodding my body.

All I want is to wake up. I've got to find Livia.

Pain propels me over the threshold of sleep and into waking. Another prison cell. Not a sugar coated version like at the Institute. Brick walls and a door made of steel bars cage me.

The fiery throbbing on the left side of my body calls, I remember now I was shot. The bullet entered below the collarbone. White bandages wrap my shoulder and encircle my chest covering my breasts. To hold my arm immobile, a bandage fuses my arm to my side at the elbow. The wound itches and I scratch at it absentmindedly. I realize too late it is going to hurt, except it doesn't.

I got shot, why doesn't it hurt? Just a second ago it hurt like hell.

Gingerly, I peel back the bandage to look at the wound. Before my eyes, I can see it healing.

Well, that's not normal.

A pair of jeans and a tee shirt lay at the foot of the cot. Whoever the jeans belong to is close to my size. Well-worn with holes in the knees, the jeans fit comfortably, but the t-shirt is too big. I don't mind. Fitted clothing would aggravate my wound. Dressing is cumbersome, and it burns, but I manage. Utilizing my good arm, I run my hand through the tangled mess on my head.

I turn towards the door, and a man is on the other side. The guy that growled at the guard for grabbing me. My knight in shining armor, the man from the loft, close enough I could reach out and touch him. Tall, lean, and muscular, his longish and unruly hair is an earthy dark coffee color with gold highlights. His jaw is clean-shaven and he wears a pair of dark blue jeans and a grey sweater. Not glowing, so maybe I imagined it, but his green eyes are still amazing as he carefully takes me in.

Did he watch me get dressed?

He crosses his arms over his chest, widening his stance. "If you even think about trying any of your Jedi mind tricks on me I will break your neck before you can blink."

My jaw drops and I sputter, "Um, that's fair. Wait, if I'm a Jedi does that mean you believe I am one of the good guys?"

One corner of his mouth tips up. "No, it means I like Star Wars."

"Bummer." I mutter.

I make bad jokes when I am nervous. The way he is looking at me right now has my nerves on edge.

Stupid brain.

He's a werewolf, that I am sure—But different from

Alonzo. He has no aura, thus he is born, not made.

"My name is Bastien," he says. "We need to discuss what happened in Lune Rouge last night."

I take a step forward and grasp the bars. "I will tell you everything down to the last detail, promise, but first, please, how is Livia?"

"You really care about her, don't you?" He comments softly.

Tears threaten to spill over. "I do. Do what you want with me, but she needs help. The men who held us captive shot her up with a virus; it's going to kill her."

"She's sick, the fever started a few hours ago. I promise everything is being done to help her. Right now I need to get some answers from you. What the hell happened last night? Are you a witch? Is that what the blue light was?"

Retreating to the cot, I sit down gingerly to rest my aching side. "Arcana. They call the blue light Arcana. I'm no witch, that's for sure. I was given a virus like Livia. It induces mutations in the brain. I don't know about any others, but my Arcana makes a blue light when in use." I feel the heat in my cheeks.

Bastien nods, "Did the military or the government do that to you?"

"I don't know where they get their funding. Might be the president, might be from neighborhood bake sales. The place is called The Richland Institute. A psychotic asshole named Richland runs things. He has a plan to rid the world of anything not human. Arcana was designed to level the playing field. That much he told me. Clearly he's not taking into account the people he runs these experiments on might not be keen on cooperating with him."

I start at the beginning and tell him everything. He listens to every word. Halfway through my tale, I begin to pace. Bastien obviously doesn't think I am a threat because he unlocked the cell to sit on my cot some time ago. Finally, I run out of things to tell. He runs a weary hand down his face before leaning back against the bricks.

"Guess Dad was right when he said this was going to bring the Tribunal down on our heads. It will take a few hours before they're all assembled. You are going to need to repeat what you told me to the Council. For what it is worth, I believe you." Sympathy warms his eyes. I could look at them all day, but I am worried about what he just said.

"Tribunal? Council? What are those?" I ask.

"Governing bodies. The Tribunal is comprised of the heads of each house for all the major families, packs, vampire clans, covens, and Fae courts."

The United Nations of the not quite human?

"The Council is therian community only," he says.

"Where does the word therian come from?"

"Therian is short for therianthropy, which is the metamorphosis of a man into an animal. It is an all-encompassing word for any species of shape shifters. We don't like the term werewolf."

"Great. I am just learning to handle the idea of werewolves, and now you throw vampires and fairies my way," I huff.

"Fae," he corrects.

"Whatever."

He has the nerve to laugh. "Baby, you have no idea what you just got cast into. Therians and vampires are the bulk of the Tribunal in this region. The others rarely show up. Witches are too human to care about our problems. Fae are stuck up. They live on an alternate plane of existence parallel to ours. If it does not happen over there, we're not likely to see them."

Soberly I ask, "How much trouble am I in?"

His sigh is heavy and brings me no relief. "Humans want to use you as a weapon, right?"

"Yes, but don't I get points for foiling their evil plan?" I murmur.

"You already cashed that favor in otherwise you'd be dead right now. The vote barely went in favor of keeping you alive long enough to find out what you know."

"What are my chances?" I demand.

"I won't lie, they're slim. I intend to talk to my dad about vouching for you. He's the alpha over all the other wolf packs. It gives him influence in political matters."

The Council or Tribunal may decide to kill me, but surely Livia will not be considered a threat.

Would they kill a child?

"What about Livia? They won't hurt her, will they? She's only five, how dangerous can she be?"

Bastien sighs. "That's a little more difficult. Did you know she's not human?"

"I noticed she was different, but hadn't had time to figure

out what she is." I answer, surprised.

"She's half wolf therian. My older brother Athan went missing over a decade ago. Many have disappeared through the years. Madalaina and I both noticed his scent on the girl last night. Tests are being run, but they're only a formality. She's Athan's daughter. Her mother's side of the family is where things become interesting." He sounds bitter. "Winter, the Fae bartender from Lune Rouge, says Livia is a Royal Red Fae. If it is true, then she has a hard road ahead of her."

"What's a Royal Red?" I question.

"The Dawn Court, also called the Summer Court or Seelie Court, of Fairy has a particular genetic quirk that runs through the females of the high royals, flaming red hair. Winter swears Livia's one. Turns out they had a princess go missing soon after Athan. Only she turned up dead later. Rumor was she had given birth, but no one expected the child lived since ransom was never demanded."

Overwhelmed I plop down next to Bastien on the cot. "This is all too much. My headache's worse than before."

He looks at me and brushes the hair off my forehead. "Who gave you the bruise over your right eye? A gift from The Richland Institute?"

"A gift from the guards, to be exact. Rifle butt hit me. It was a pretty nasty cut before."

Warily, he touches the bruise making me wince. "Sorry. Looks better than it did earlier. The Arcana you told me about might be helping you heal faster. I hope the guy that hit you is one of the two assholes I killed," he snarled. I have no trouble imagining Bastien with blood on his hands. He has lethal predator written all over him. I'm briefly reminded of Alonzo.

"Oh God. Will I be charged with the death of Alonzo?"

I try to get up to pace again, but Bastien catches me around the waist and pulls me on to his lap. "I will keep you safe. Trust me to protect you."

I shouldn't let him touch me so intimately, but it feels nice to have someone be tender with me.

The magnetism I felt from his stare last night is stronger when he touches me.

"What is going to happen to me?" I whisper. "Shifters don't frown on murder?"

Bastien takes hold of my chin and forces me to meet his gaze. "What you described isn't murder."

Relieved, I hug Bastien's neck. He gives me hope and I've been without hope for a long time. There is something about him that pulls me in. It could be his kindness or the eyes that warm me to my soul. I lift my head from his shoulder and my lips are drawn to his. I meant it to be a chaste touching of lips. Brief and passionless; to show gratitude. When our lips touch a spark flickers to life. His lips move gently under mine. My hand trails to his smooth cheek. He teases the hem of my shirt up just a fraction to stroke my side exceptional attention to the pulse at the base of my throat. Sharp teeth nip at the skin.

"What is that scent you're wearing?" Bastien asks me.

I shake my head. "I'm not wearing any perfume."

Bastien and I are kissing again, deeper this time. It's more intimate than anything I've experience with a man in the past. I've had sex once before.

What an epic fail.

I decided to fly solo until I found a better reason not to. Bastien is better than any fantasy I ever had.

"Ahem. Perhaps you can find a better time and place for this, son."

Wrapped up in each other, Bastien and I didn't hear his father approaching. I want to shrink away, but Bastien won't let me hide. I am wrapped around him like a vine, and he won't allow me to let go.

"We'll be up in a minute, Dad."

"Don't make me wait too long, Bastien." His footsteps recede up the stairs.

Alone again, Bastien chuckles against my neck. I jump off his lap.

"Well that was embarrassing!" I cry. He arches an eyebrow at me. "The kiss was out of this world. Your father walking in is not something I needed at this moment. Aren't you worried?"

"Not particularly." Bastien reaches up and holds out his hand to me, "Wanna meet my family?"

Sure, why not?

CHAPTER 8

Rachel

BASTIEN LEADS ME UPSTAIRS to his father's study. Claude Bonvillian introduces himself from behind a tremendous wooden desk. Its size emphasizes how big he is. He assesses me as we near the chairs in front of the desk.

"Well Rachel, you've made quite the impression in such a short time. Especially on my son, I see" He smiles a little, putting me at ease.

"That was a misunderstanding. I mean it wasn't supposed to happen. I couldn't help myself; I mean look at him. Oh God." I'm mortified but Bastien is amused. His hand is in front of his mouth, and he's shaking with suppressed laughter.

"She's cute, son. I understand your fascination with her. Happy as I am to see my boy take a serious interest in a woman, we're short on time. You brought my granddaughter home; I will forever be grateful to you for that. If you're going to survive the scrutiny of the Council, you need to learn Therian's laws before tonight. My daughter Madalaina will go over protocol and teach you all she can."

"Dad, I can teach protocol," Bastien protests.

"I think she will learn more with Madalaina. Fewer

distractions."

Bastien opens his mouth to argue again when a blonde girl bounces into the room popping bubble gum.

"He has a point big brother. I won't be tempted to kiss her." She gives him a cheeky grin. Bastien narrows his eyes at his sibling. Claude smoothly cuts off his son before he can say anything. He points Bastien out of the room. I'm nervous without him beside me.

Madalaina reclines in Bastien's empty chair with her legs draped over the armrest. "Just us girls now."

"Relax. I'm here to help you." She pops her gum in between sentences.

"How'd you know we kissed?"

"Smell. You smell like Bastien. Scent marking."

I didn't think it possible, but I'm even more flustered.

The carefree girl facade slips for a second and I can see the mature woman underneath. "I would love to relax and gab with you for hours, learn everything there is to know about Rachel, but if you don't pick up what I teach you fast, I doubt you will live long enough for us to get that chance. I love Bastien. Something big is brewing between you two and I won't let him lose a chance at something great. We need to get to work." Madalaina slides back into the effervescent girl in a blink. "You're about to get a crash course in all things shape-shifter. To my knowledge no human has ever been told so much without already having a therian mate. You my friend are unique."

Madalaina talks for the next three hours. Therians

descend from Cain, as in biblical Cain and Abel. Therianthropy is a curse inflicted upon Cain for killing Abel. Act like an animal become an animal. The local shape-shifter community consists of wolves, vipers, grizzlies, and one lion. Apparently, Taka, the dragon I met in the tank, is a whole different creature. A handful of dragons remain in the city as foreign dignitaries. Dragos, the proper name for the dragons, were cursed as well, but by the Fae. Madalaina wouldn't say much more about the Fae other than they're not friendly. She tells me if I want to know more about the Fae, I can ask Winter.

After the history lesson, she broke down the hierarchy. At the very top is the Alpha Prime. He rules over each shape-shifter without exception. The Alpha of all alphas. Usually that sort of strength runs in families, but it is not unheard of for someone outside the bloodline to challenge. Claude was the current prime. He had expected Athan to lead after him, but with his disappearance it has been unclear who will succeed him. Madalaina said Bastien is far too laid back to be Prime. I think she's wrong. The Bastien I met was pretty intense.

Beyond the Prime, is the elite. The warriors. They're the strongest and fastest. Betas follow, a class of average citizens. Children, elderly, injured, or impaired individuals are considered omegas. They're protected and taken care of. Human mates occasionally happen, though it is discouraged. They fall in the omega class as impaired.

Turning a person into a shifter is outlawed and punishable by death unless you have permission from the Prime. Humans live as long as their spouse in a mated pair, so most couples don't bother. The problem with turning a human is they cannot control their shift during the full moon.

According to the law, fighting is allowed only in front of the Prime or Council. Unsanctioned fights required enough eyewitnesses to convince the Council it was unavoidable or those involved would face retribution. An injured party could request the Council issue a weregild or man price, paid in possessions and flesh. Weregilds are severe consequences as they're capable of bankrupting or even becoming a death sentence.

Madalaina guides me to her bedroom upstairs to find sufficient clothes. She's a few inches taller and slimmer than me, so pants are out. She draws out a white dress with little sparkly crystals on the front from her closet. The dress belongs in a club, not a courtroom. I glance at Madalaina askance. She takes one look at my furrowed brown and chuckles.

"Try it." She responds. "I know it's not ideal, but white will help you seem innocent, everything else I own is a bad idea. I buy my clothing to drive Adele crazy." She insouciantly falls on her stomach across the bed.

"Who's Adele?"

"Mother dearest. Athan disappeared when I was ten. She stopped being a devoted mother and decided her remaining children were not as important as the golden boy. Mom and I aren't on speaking terms, at least civilly, most of the year."

I did the math in my head; if she were ten when Athan disappeared that would make her at minimum twenty years old now.

I study myself in the mirror; the dress does look nice on me.

I don't have as much to work with as Madalaina in the chest department. The straps are about an inch wide, and the hem hits mid-thigh. Even though I was blessed with a naturally tan complexion, I still look sallow from my time in Richland.

When was the last time I spent any time in the sun?

My eyes are hazel and maybe a little squinty. I think I qualify as cute rather than beautiful with my high cheekbones and dimples, they fit perfectly with my ready smile.

Used to be a ready smile, haven't had a reason to smile in ages.

Madalaina assists me in removing the bandages. The bullet wound is substantially healed.

At least Arcana is useful for something.

We elect to leave the big bandages off and place smaller gauze over the wound.

My hair is limp and heavy, lacking style. A honey blonde, the highlights give it a warm glow that I think makes it my best feature. Turns out, Madalaina has a gift with hair. She whipped out a set of scissors, and in moments soft layers frame my face and fall to mid-back.

The last item she gives me is a pair of conservative heels.

Madalaina hugs me. "Alright. Time to go face the music."

A green SUV is idling in front of the house. Bastien leans against the driver's side. His pants are black, and the white button down shirtsleeves are rolled up above the elbow, the dark waves of his hair kiss the collar. His grin is roguish. I'm witnessing the playful Bastien Madalaina spoke of. Madalaina skips down the steps and climbs into the backseat. Bastien takes me by the hand around to the passenger seat.

"You don't need to open doors for me." I assure him.

"And waste the chance to hold your hand?"

He keeps my hand for the whole trip. I have limited experience with men, but I get things are escalating fast. I like him, and if I had more time I would object to his forwardness, but as it stands, I may be dead in an hour. This could be the last time anyone offers me affection. With a heavy heart, I think of the plans I had. Graduate from college, get a job, and fall head over heels in love. Eventually, we would marry and have children. I can't see any of that happening now. Provided the Council lets me live, what then? I will need to run and spend the rest of my life in hiding. Bastien's interest in me will wane. All alone with my Arcana, I can't imagine any other future.

CHAPTER 9

Cleary

DAMN MEETINGS.

The others don't want me on the Council, but I am the sole alpha werecat within a hundred miles. Claude exercised my minority status to force my compliance. I'd rather laze around. It is my nature after all. Male lions aren't known for being active members of the community. I said yes because I'm nosy. My headstone is apt to read 'Cleary Neil. Curiosity kills another cat.' Today's dispute is over a human woman. She caused a big stink by taking out an anti-were group. Based on the account I was told, we should be presenting this girl with a medal. Instead everyone is freaking over how dangerous she is.

I'm bored already.

Time to chill out behind my sunglasses. Another perk of being a lion, not many are dense enough to cross you. I relax behind the table and wait for something exciting to happen. I don't have to wait long. Bastien accompanies the woman and his sister, Madalaina, into the assembly gallery. The space looks like a fight club crammed to the rafters with spectators. The center arena is used by the accused to defend themself, at times physically. Bleachers fan out in a circle. I sit up on the platform with the additional five Council leaders. Claude and his wife Adele are in the middle. The man on Claude's left is a behemoth of a grizzly shifter named Jay. He dwarfs the diminutive woman close to him. I can't look at her without shivering. A viper as cold-hearted, as she's cold blooded. Next to me is the Dragos, Aoto He's a reptile, too, but I like him. The old coot is a riot at parties.

"The accused has entered. Let's begin." Claude calls out to the room.

The female is standing in the arena alone. I can hear her heart pounding in her chest.

Poor thing is terrified. She looks harmless to me.

"Rachel Ryan, by your own confession, you are guilty of killing a werewolf from our pack. You entered a shifter establishment with the intent to destroy us. Yet you didn't. You betrayed your own, and supplied us information about this Richland Institute that may prove vital to the future survival of our species. The answer is not clear. A vote will be taken. We start with Lyssa."

"Ssshe isss a human with too much power. I sssay kill her now to sssave the time later."

Told you she's a cold-hearted bitch.

"Jay, your vote?"

The grizzly leans back in his chair. It groans under his hefty weight. "She seems too weak to be able to tear a beast right out of a man. I wouldn't buy it if my Uncle Earl hadn't seen her at the bar. He told me how she tried to protect that little girl. Let her live. She's as much of a victim as anyone else." Jay pushes away from the table and leaves. He did his part.

He has as much use for Council business as me.

"Adele, my love? How charitable are you feeling?"

She snorts delicately. "She's of no use to me. She returned a half-breed grandchild, and by the smell of her she wants to snare my son and produce more mongrels. I won't allow it."

I've often wondered how Claude keeps Adele from eating her young. I look over to Madalaina standing next to her brother. She's glaring daggers at her mother. Bastien seems calm, but his eyes reveal a different story. Unlike Madalaina, who is an open book, Bastien shows the world only what he wants them to see. How odd for him to be so easy for me to read.

"Cleary, yes or no?"

I push my sunglasses on top of my head before speaking. "This whole affair is a bullshit display of power. You and I know it, Claude. She defended herself. I can't blame her for that."

Madalaina is gawking at me. I wink at her. She frowns. Claude scowls at me. Big papa doesn't worry me. If I were to desire the little temptress, her father can't dissuade me. The fact that he commands the entire therian army gives me pause. Flirting with Madalaina is innocent. Dating her could be perilous.

Claude focuses on the Dragos. Thumbs up from Fu Man Chu.

"Grizzly, Lion, and Dragos support the human. Snake does not. I vote in favor of Rachel. She lives. Miss Ryan will be delivered into protective custody." Claude rises but is frozen by vicious shouting.

"The bitch has to die. She murdered my son!" The mother of the man Rachel killed rises. "I will avenge my child!"

Behind her is Alonzo's brother. He puts his arm around his mother to comfort her. "Don't cry Mama. I will get justice for Alonzo." He turns towards the Council and yells, "I demand weregild from Rachel Ryan!"

Out of nowhere, Bastien is beside Rachel, his hand on her arm as he whispers in her ear.

"Uh, I want Bastien as my champion!" Rachel blurts out as Bastien starts to unbutton his shirt.

Miguel just bit off a lot more than he can chew.

Bastien is a fun loving kind of guy. He's easy to laugh, always joking, but he's also the son of the Alpha Prime. He was taught to fight brutally from the cradle.

"Bastien, son, you are familiar with the law. She's not our kin, nor mate to our kin. We have no ties to this woman. You cannot champion a stranger." Claude reminds him.

Claude is a slick one. Every word he says is carefully measured. There was something in there meant for Bastien to grasp. Father and son stare at one another. Bastien snakes a hand around Rachel's waist and leans her backward until she's flush against him. His right palm is flat on her abdomen. He tilts her head to the side with his left.

"Then I claim her." His teeth sink into the flesh of Rachel's neck.

Adele rages. I want to cheer. The claiming bite done, Bastien whirls Rachel around to face him, his lips crash down on hers. Must be some kiss because Bastien has to hold her up. When the kiss ends, he barks at Madalaina for help. She takes her brother's mate out of his embrace and carries her to the nearby benches. Bastien is in the ring, chest and feet bare. When he lost the shoes, I don't know.

The man is faster than the flash when he puts his mind to it.

Rachel's blood still marks his lips and chin. "Come on, Miguel. You want blood. Let's shed blood."

Miguel sneers and leaves with his Mama.

Bastien faces his father. "She has been blooded. By the morning, she will be bedded."

Damn, now I'm jealous.

Claude nods, "The law doesn't accept her as a full mate until then."

Madalaina hugs her new sister in law. "You'll be okay, Rachel. I know you're confused but trust Bastien. He will take care of you."

She moves back while Bastien collects his bride. His shirt is on but unbuttoned. I follow Madalaina out into the front hall. She stands gazing out the window. Her brow is furrowed. She's cute when she worries.

I put a hand on her shoulder to comfort her. "It'll be okay Mads."

She jumps, startled. "Damn it, Cleary! Don't sneak up on people. They should staple a bell to you. And stop calling me Mads."

I snicker. "Sure thing Mads. Are you going to be okay?"

"Hell no. Bastien just claimed a mate, I'm thrilled for him, but Mom is gonna be a nightmare. Dad is maintaining a vigilant eye on the niece I never knew I had. Which leaves me to bear the brunt of Mom's tirade. It's going to be of epic proportions, I assure you. I ordinarily crash at Bastien's house when she gets like that, but he'll have enough to work out right now without having his little sister underfoot." She's animated when she talks, hands waving all over the place.

"You're welcome at my apartment." I offer.

"Cleary Neil I am not a notch on anyone's bedpost." She punches me in the arm.

Rubbing the spot I say, "Whoa! I didn't say you were. If you need a place to hide out, you got one. On the couch, relax."

"Oh. Okay. Um, thanks. If she gets too atrocious, I might come by. I better get going. Maybe I can get home and lock myself in my room before she gets there."

I watch her leave. Madalaina is a good girl. I pray to God that I am mated before she fully comes into her own.

Otherwise, I am a complete goner.

CHAPTER 10

Rachel

WHAT THE HELL JUST HAPPENED!? *What did he mean he 'claimed' me?*

Bastien has a lot of explaining to do. The biting thing wasn't bad, but I shouldn't have almost orgasmed from a flesh wound. I sense him before I see him approaching. Bastien seats himself on the bench touching me. He's tying his shoes.

"Does your neck hurt?" He won't look at me.

I touch the bite. "Not much, maybe a little tender. Miguel wanted to rip my throat out. In comparison, this is excellent."

He sweeps me up into his arms. Sharp green eyes stare into mine. "Don't compare me to him. We're nothing alike."

I lift my hand to cup his cheek. "I know you aren't. I don't understand how, but I know." He hugs me closer. I lay my head against him listening to his breathing.

He doesn't say anything. We head for his car. He deposits me in the passenger seat, even belts me in. Tenderly he pushes my hair over my shoulder. "I love your hair. The color, it's like gold." Bastien rubs a strand between his fingers. "What happened in there, I don't expect you to understand. I promise to explain and answer all your questions. Have patience with me?"

He hasn't given me any reason not to trust him. There is no denying that I am drawn to him, and the idea of being with him doesn't scare me. Taking a deep breath, I give him a timid smile. "I can do patience if you can."

He rewards me with a smile of his own. "I will be a good mate, Rachel."

We don't talk on the drive to Bastien's house. We're both still trying to process. Bastien was a bachelor this morning. Now he has a wife, mate, whatever. Still, it sounds so final. I remain apprehensive about the whole, 'She will be bedded by morning,' comment.

Bastien lives in the nicer section of town. A subdivision with wooded lots; all of the houses have extra acreage to give it a rural feel. Bastien parks his SUV in the garage. We enter the house through the kitchen. It connects to a dining room, and a living room with a large flat screen TV and several game consoles—guy stuff. Upstairs are three bedrooms. One is used as an office. The other was set up as a spare for company. A woman's touch is evident in the decor.

"Madalaina sleeps here a lot."

A far cry from the girlish decorations I saw earlier today at the Bonvillian house. The two bedrooms are as different as night and day. Madalaina is a puzzle I want to solve. Which room represents Madalaina and which is a mask? The twinge of jealousy I get when I observe so many feminine objects is squelched. I'm already attached to him. I know we ought to get to the business of sealing the deal, so to speak. Bastien must sense my indecision because he steers me towards the master bedroom with a hand to the small of my back.

"Would you like to shower? You still have blood on your neck."

I give him a stiff nod. In the bathroom, the glass and tile shower remind me of the testing tank. I start shaking.

PTSD, anyone?

Bastien wants to hug me, but I put my hand out between us. I am not ready to fall apart yet. If he closes those arms around me, I will be lost. He respects my need for distance and leaves.

I undress and step into the shower. The warm water runs over my body washing the tension away. I am alive and safe. With Bastien by my side, I will find some way to carve out a new life. My worst fear is that I'm going to wake up and be back in the Institute. The shower door opens, and a naked Bastien steps in. The muscles in his chest and stomach are neatly defined. Bastien has a large fleur-de-lis tattoo on his right shoulder over his bicep.

"I tried to stay away. I couldn't last any longer. The need to mate now that I've marked you is overwhelming."

He needs me. His face tells me he's afraid I will reject him. Instead, I press myself against him.

Bastien strokes my back lazily. "Your bandage is falling off, I can see the bullet wound is healed. Too good actually. That's unreal for a human."

"Really? I noticed it was doing a lot better when I woke up. Is it completely healed now?" I ask concerned.

"The hole from the bullet is closed up. It'll probably scar, I can't say for sure with the Arcana. It's an angry red, but seems to be healthy. Does it hurt?"

Experimentally I rotate my arm. "No. It's stiff, but there's no pain."

"We should probably get you cleaned up before we use up all the hot water in the house. Turn around."

He washes my hair then starts on my body. His soapy hands are on my shoulders and work down my back; massaging away every ache. After he finishes with my back, I feel his slick palms slide across my skin to my front. Bastien traces small circles on my breasts with his fingertips. The circles grow a fraction every revolution but never touch the nipple. When he runs a finger on the underside of my right breast, I gasp. My nipples beg to be touched, but he ignores them. The ache between my legs is worse than the one growing in my breasts. Bastien's right hand wanders down my ribcage and around to my stomach. He swirls around my belly button before journeying downward to the apex of my thighs. My knees weaken. He divides my folds, teasing the most sensitive part of my body. A shiver rolls through me.

"So responsive." His lips tease the shell of my ear. "I can't wait to get my mouth on you. I want to hear you scream for me."

His fingers work me until I'm on the brink of orgasm. His hand moves to plunge into my heat. My head drops back, I closed my eyes and cry out. He doesn't stop or pull his finger free until the last ripple of my orgasm subsides. Bastien's lips linger on the mark where he bit me. I tilt my head to look at him. His green eyes are so bright they glow; fangs grow longer in his mouth. A shiver escapes me under the intensity of his stare.

His gaze turns predatory. He twists the knob for the water off. I walk out of the shower and towards the bed, looking over my shoulder once to check if he's following. Bastien is on my heels. I crawl onto the bed. He flips me to my back and follows me down. Leaning up I meet his lips halfway. He nips at my bottom lip and parts my mouth with is tongue, deepening the kiss.. Passion consumes me.

He breaks the kiss with a groan and lays his forehead against mine. "I need to slow down. I don't want to hurt you, but damn I want you so bad I burn."

"I'm tougher than I look."

He laughs. "I noticed."

"I want you too, Bastien. I'm sure slow is swell, and we should try it sometime, but I'm on fire too. I need you. I think I will die if I don't have you."

"It's the mate bond. I didn't know if it would affect you the same way."

"Please, Bastien. I trust you."

With his knee, he nudges my legs wider and settles between them. His fingers dip into me.

"God, you're so wet."

He positions himself, I can feel him begin to enter me. I peer down my body at his dusky uncircumcised cock. It twitches under my perusal. With one last look for reassurance he slides into me. My gasp meets his moan. A lack of experience on my part and his girth make for a tight fit. He gives me a minute to adjust. His first thrust brings me halfway to orgasm. I shove my fingers into his hair and hold on. The more worked up I get, the more I can feel the Arcana buzzing in my blood.

Now's not the best time.

Each stroke hits me deeper. He builds speed and I arched up off the bed. Bastien latches onto my right breast with his mouth. It sends me crashing into another orgasm. He thrusts two more times and I feel him shudder over me. He buries himself to the hilt and presses his forehead between my breasts. Bastien waits to catch his breath before he moves to kiss me slowly but passionately. A content sigh escapes him against my lips as he breaks contact.

"Oh God, Rachel. I don't think my heart can take what you do to me." His head rests in the crook of my neck.

The mention of hearts is sobering. Bastien and I are not in love. He didn't choose me because he wanted me. Some misguided sense of duty forced him to mate me. If I'm not careful, I will fall hard. My heart needs protection from itself.

CHAPTER 11

Subject #634860

SOMETHING BIG HAPPENED. I don't know what transpired, but everyone is on edge. Richland is driving me harder than normal. In all the wasted years I've been locked up, they have never been so panicked. The medical personnel are always frightened of me, but this isn't about me. Whoever caused all this trouble, I hope they keep it up. I need the distraction. If I can avert the focus off me long enough, I might finally be ready to move. Planning and waiting. Patience is a virtue. I must restrain myself. I will break out. Then they will pay in blood. I intend to bathe in it. I will crush my enemies and leave a trail of corpses behind me.

CHAPTER 12

Winter

I DON'T BELONG HERE.

Truthfully, I don't belong anywhere. As a fairy born of both Courts, I am trapped between them. My name was given to me as a reminder of my dual citizenship.

A slap in the face is more like it.

Winter Summersun. My mother is the daughter of the Summer Queen. She's a Royal Red with the trademark flaming red hair. My father was the bastard of the Winter King. Their brief dalliance resulted in me. The Royal Red gene combined with dad's Dusk Court white blond produced my lavender hair. Mom says my hair is my first failure. I'm on the record of successors to both dominions, but I will never sit on either throne.

I hate being in Fairy.

Before Dad died, I had a place to stay, where I felt someone wanted me.

Dad knew what it was like to be unwanted.

At his funeral, I threw a fit when Mom said that she was happy to be rid of him. You can't scream and cuss at a Royal Red in public, even if she's your mother. She had me banished from Fairy. I'm happy living in the mortal realm, but the binding of my Fae magic is painful. Magic is part of the Fae, like breathing. I've been suffocating going on three years now.

I wish Tsura and Madalaina were here with me.

I could use their support right now, but they would be even less welcome in Fairy than me. I'm here to petition on behalf of Livia Bonvillian. If I had not called in some huge favors, I would have been executed for trespassing. Banished Fae aren't allowed to visit for any reason. Luckily, Ianthe, a Siren, owed me. I cashed in my chips to get here safely.

"Well if it isn't my favorite little rebel."

I groan. The voice belongs to Kiril, my cousin. The only family member who willingly talks to me.

I wish he wouldn't.

Kiril is a classic Summer Court Fae. Every word out of his mouth is a well-placed instrument to further his plans. Judging by the fancy clothes he's wearing I'd say he elevated his social standing since we last spoke. Nobody climbs a social ladder like Kiril.

"They sent you to punish me?"

"That hurts, really." He mocks with a hand over his heart. "You couldn't obtain anything finer to wear?"

"It wouldn't matter what I wore. Nothing mortal will reach Court standards. I can't access my magic, so I didn't bother."

I have on a gorgeous dress, but it pales in comparison to what the Court ladies are wearing. I won't lie; I miss the clothes. I loved the formal dresses. Not much call for fancy frocks bartending at the Lune Rouge.

"Banishment is a bitch, but then so is your mother," he smirks.

He would know, he grew up with her. I've heard Mom loved to torture Kiril as a child. He doesn't like her and does anything he can to piss her off.

Probably why he talks to me.

Amalia, Livia's mother, was the Aunt closest to him in age.

Quite the tangled web that wove its way into my life last night.

"Preaching to the choir," I mumble.

"Come on, you were only granted limited time for an audience. Your Grandmother is waiting." Kiril turns and leads me to the Queen.

The butterflies in my stomach are on fire. I follow Kiril to the throne room. I want to run and hide. My grandmother has flayed people alive in the dining room for not laughing at her jokes. A pair of gilt doors open, and I stand in front of my family. My Grandmother, mother, and aunts all sit prepared to judge me.

"Queen Tanith, I present your granddaughter. Princess Winter Summersun." Kiril tries to put flare into the introduction. It falls flat.

She looks unimpressed. "What are you wearing? Did you hope I would kill you on the spot? I don't need another bloody martyr. Get her out Kiril."

"My Queen, Winter is banished. Her wardrobe was not meant to offend. Her magic was bound in order to pay penance for crimes against her mother. All who view her recognize she's lowly and not worth compassion."

She's his grandmother too and he calls her My Queen. Our

family is messed up.

Grandmother is pleased. "All right Kiril. You campaigned hard for her five minutes. She may have them."

Kiril bartered for my audience? What does he want out of this?

"I wish to bring the Court's attention to a lost Fae. The child of Amalia was discovered. She's suffering and needs healing."

Tanith looks mildly interested. "Who is the child's father?"

"A Lycan noble, the eldest son of the Alpha Prime, Athan Bonvillian."

Play up the royal angle.

"An illegitimate half Lycan? I doubt my Amalia would want me to claim such a creature in her name." Tanith sneers disdainfully.

"She's Royal Red. She's her mother's mirror." I plead.

"She has no place here. Neither do you."

Thank goodness for small favors. I wouldn't want to fit in around here.

She dismisses me. I look at my mother, but she won't make eye contact.

Fine. I will find help elsewhere.

Kiril steers me out of the throne room with a hand on my shoulder. Out of hearing distance, he says to me, "I'm sorry, Winter. I had hoped her love for Amalia would make a difference. In my heart, I knew she would never go for it." He's saddened by his own admission.

"I was stupid to think she would care."

"Shh! Not so loud! Do you want to die?" Kiril pulls me quickly away from prying ears.

"Why did you get me the hearing? You don't expect me to believe you care what happens to the girl?" I ask him sarcastically.

"You don't know nearly as much as you would like to think you do. Mother is right; she has no place here. Doesn't mean she should die. You're Fae on both sides, but your dual Court status makes you unpopular. What kind of life would a half Lycan child endure here? Amalia had a kind heart. She wouldn't condemn her own child."

He's right, damn it.

"I barely remember Amalia." I whisper. "She was kind to me. I remember she would sing to me when I was afraid at night. Mother would berate her for it, but she did it anyway."

"She was a sweet woman and she paid a price for it. No one treated her right and she was too easy to take advantage of. Her mistakes are how I learned if you are soft in Fairy, you will be a victim." Kiril looks at the floor pensively.

"You should come meet your cousin."

"I can't. If she really looks just like Amalia, I can't. Look, seek out the vampire doctor, he knows many things. He's been around since time immemorial."

Vampires? Does he want to get me killed?

"He won't see me. Vampires hate the Fae almost as much as the Fae hate them."

"And with good reason. Here, take this," he mutters as he slips a tome into my coat pocket.

I chuckle. "A book? Since when do you carry books

around?"

Kiril isn't the studious type. He's more the handsome playboy without an intelligent thought in his head.

"Are you always such a smartass? I figured since the queen wouldn't lift a finger to help the ailing child of my dearly departed cousin I would have to do something. If you ever tell anyone I gave you the book, I will swear I never saw it in my life. You'll be executed if they learn you have it. Guard it well. After you read it, you will know how to get an audience with the doctor. In the mean time, I'll work on a backup plan just in case."

CHAPTER 13

July 6

Varian

I LOVE FAIRIES. *For dinner.*

Most vampires think Fae blood tastes like shit. They avoid it at all costs. It isn't bad, a bit off compared to other species. The flavor isn't what I like. The magic is. I can feel the magic humming inside as I drink. Truth is I fucking despise fairies. Pain in the ass is all they are.

This one at the door is sensational, especially with that pastel purple hair. Her eyes are a darker shade than her hair and I'm speechless, lost in their depth.

Which Court does she belong to with hair such a color? Dawn or Dusk?

Winter or Dusk Court consists of all brunettes with a smattering of pale hair. Ironic that the unsavory, Unseelie royalty are known for innocent white hair. Summer or Seelie Court only have damn redhead twits and raven haired Fae.

The first Fae I ever fed off didn't survive. Purely by accident. I was young and still learning my strength. She was a red head. Caused quite a ruckus when I took the body home.

I was being a gentleman, bringing back their stinking carcass and they try to kill me.

Turns out dinner was actually some sort of princess.

Damn, there are over fifty princesses. Were they really going to miss one?

Anyway, the crazy bitch queen sent some troops after me and I learned I was the most powerful vampire. Not to brag, but I am the shit. I sent the Fae army back to her as dust in a jar. No one told me I was a super vampire. Some shit about if I didn't know I couldn't hurt anyone. Proud to say no accidental murders committed by me in centuries. No, all my kills since then are entirely on purpose. The Fae attack me every so often. Those deaths are the most satisfying.

The woman on my doorstep reminds me of that first Fae experience. She had been looking for bed sport.

What is this one looking for? I'm torn. Do I want this woman to be another assassin or just want me for my body? Is it wrong if I want both?

Brave little firefly; showing up on a vampire's doorstep. Currently, vampires and the Fae are in a cease-fire. Manias Artorias, the Vampire Regis, negotiated it at the beginning of his reign.

Life has been painfully boring since then.

"Is this the home of Dr. Keller?" She asks.

She's looking for Keller? Disappointed, I nod and say, "He lives here, but the house belongs to Varian Caina."

Her eyes bug out. "Varian Caina? He's not home, is he?" She asks nervously.

She knows my name and reputation but has no clue what I look like? This should be fun. Instead of telling her 'Yes, you're talking to him' I lie and say "No."

Don't want to scare off the entertainment.

"Oh good." She looks relieved. "Can you please take me to the doctor? I must speak with him."

"What the hell," I shrug. "Been a while since I did anything to piss him off."

The puzzled look on her face is familiar. I get that look a lot from people. When you are more powerful than any one person should be, you seldom hear the word no. It breeds tedium. I like to catch people off guard. I think the general consensus is I'm bat shit crazy, but who is going to do anything to me? The Regis?

Yeah right. I was supposed to be the king.

Too much work so I turned the job down.

If I ever decide I want to wear a tiara, I'll just remove Manias' head and take his crown. He's lucky he's my best friend.

I take her hand and pull her along behind me. "Come on firefly, the mad scientist is this way."

"Firefly? What the hell does that mean?" She demands.

I ignore her. "Keller! A visitor has come calling," I taunt in a singsong voice.

"Who, Varian? You know I don't like visitors." The voice comes from down the hall but gets louder as we move closer to his office.

Her eyes darts to me, "Why did he call you Varian?" Her voice is suspicious.

Shrugging, I screw up my face and draw an imaginary circle with a finger next to my ear making the universal sign someone is crazy.

We reach Keller's office. Not taking my eyes off her I say, "A little Fae chit. Quite the attractive little morsel. No idea why she would want to see a mean old bastard like you, but who understands women?" She glares at me. I can't stop the goofy grin from splitting my face. Must have shown a little too much fang 'cause firefly tugs harder to free her captured hand.

Keller doesn't look up from his papers. "Fae. No use for any Fae whether they're beautiful or not. Send her away."

Well done, Keller. He's such a bastard he makes me look like a gentlemen.

Firefly approaches Keller's desk. She's not going to leave. Slamming her hands down on the surface of the desk she gets Keller's attention.

But does she really want it?

"Doctor Keller, I came to ask for your help. A hybrid Fae-Lycan child is dying. Humans poisoned her with something unknown."

"Humans, Fae, therian; what a headache," Keller mumbles, he looks back down.

Leaning against the doorframe I add my two cents worth. "Keller, if I were you I wouldn't." The girl turns her furious eyes on me. "What? Those are three factions a vampire has no cause to bother with. Why would you expect any help from us?"

It's the harsh truth whether she wants to hear it or not.

"First of all, I didn't ask for *your* help, I asked for his. Second, she's a child. And last, no matter how much the doctor wants to forget, he has ties to the Fae Court as does every vampire in existence."

I'm sorry, repeat that last part again?

Keller gets up, just a breath separates him from the little firefly. "Do you even know what you are talking about? I pray you don't, because if you do your life is forfeited. Neither monarch will let you live with such knowledge."

Her chin raises a fraction. "I can take care of myself."

Keller scoffs at her and I laugh.

Defiant beauty, I like her.

She narrows her eyes at both us. "You're okay with a child dying when you might be able to help her?"

"You must be a very young Fae. When you have lived as long as I, one more death won't bother you." Keller dismisses.

I have to disagree. Kids aren't the same as ancient old farts like Keller.

Angrily, she asks, "So you don't care who dies around you?"

She's not talking to me, but I answer the questions anyway. "I don't really care if I die. At least I would be doing something different."

Keller gathers an armful of books and papers. "If you two would shut up I'm ready to go. Take me to the girl."

She smiles and does an honest-to-god happy dance. This Fae is delightful.

So glad I didn't eat her.

I grab my coat. No way am I missing this. "I haven't been near any Lycans in ages. This is going to be a blast."

"Oh no, you are not coming." She stops dead in her tracks.

I laugh harder than I have all year. I want her to stick around. Firefly amuses the hell outta me. "You couldn't stop me if you had an army."

She cocks her head to the side and looks at me thoughtfully. "You're Varian, aren't you? I don't get it. Why is everyone afraid of you? I agree you're odd and quite possibly off your meds, but you don't seem dangerous."

I smile innocently. "I'm as harmless as a church mouse. Don't know where they got the idea I am the boogeyman." Keller scoffs. I ignore him like always and say to her, "Now move that cute little ass before I decide to keep you."

CHAPTER 14

Bastien

RACHEL IS SLEEPING on the bed beside me. My mate.
How did I get a mate?
I'm usually not the commitment type. What possessed me to claim this human woman for the rest of my life? Now that we're mated, her life is bound to mine. Her life span just jumped into the triple digits.

There is no denying Rachel is beautiful. I noticed her the moment she walked into Lune Rouge. Smelled her is better, scent plays a significant part in Lycan mating. Probably in all therian mating, but I couldn't swear to it. Rachel smells like shelter. I noticed it down in the cells when I first spoke to her. It's intoxicating. This leads me to believe she was already destined to be mine.

Fate

My mate and my lost brother's child somehow walk into my world together. Twenty-four hours later I've bound myself permanently to her, and am seriously considering adopting my niece. It appears Rachel has bonded to Livia as if she were her own daughter.

Perhaps she won't mind being a wife and mother overnight?

The bedding has fallen below her navel. Blonde hair drifts

across the pillows. A lock of hair lay over her left breast, winding around the gentle slope. I pursue the swirl of spun gold around to her nipple before palming the whole breast. She stirs in her sleep. My hand travels between her breasts. Gradually I skim my palm down stomach. Rachel is slim, but not gaunt. Her abdomen has a slight roundness; her hips and breasts are full. Generous proportions instead of the skeletal frame that's popular today.

My hand slips below the sheet, carrying it with me. Short, blonde curls conceal velvet heat. I spread my fingers through the hairs until I find her slit. Dipping my fingers into her wet warmth I slowly roll the sensitive bud hiding amidst her curls. She's beginning to wake up. I toss back the bed sheet, and ease down the mattress to taste what my fingers have held. My lips touch the softness outside her core and I hear her gasp. Looking up her body, I meet her drowsy gaze. Sleep tousled, eyes heavy lidded with desire. I coil my arm around her waist and haul her down the bed so I can become better acquainted with her most intimate parts more comfortably. Her legs dangle off the edge, I kneel on the floor between them.

"Good morning." I smile at her. I follow up my greeting with a slow lick. Rachel tries to pull back. She looks at me with shy indecision. "Never had anyone go down on you before?"

Biting her lip, she shakes her head no.

"Hmm. Not sorry to hear that. Relax. Let your legs go free. I promise you will enjoy this. Even if I've to work at it all day."

She arches an eyebrow at me. I press my tongue into her again. I've slid my hands under her buttocks to hold her tight.

Tremors rack her body. She's close to coming. I feel her nails on the back of my head, pressing me to her. Beneath me, Rachel's body rides the waves of an orgasm. When her body quiets down I use the sheet to wipe my mouth before resting my head on her stomach. With her silky skin against my cheek and my left hand tracing the curve of her hip, I've never been more content. It's selfish of me but I want to keep her here forever. I don't care what life she had before; she's mine now. Rachel plays with my hair lazily and I drift into a euphoria I never dared believe exists.

CHAPTER 15

Winter

AN EXILED FAE PRINCESS walks into a werewolf's home with two vampires.

Sounds like a joke I was once told.

Claude is granting us permission to see his granddaughter. She may be the only piece of his son Athan left in the world. If a vampire can save her life, he will put his prejudice aside. The nursery we're taken to in Claude's home is outfitted with hospital machinery monitoring Livia's vital signs. Keller examines her, drawing tubes of blood, taking hair samples and saliva. The man had better be the genius Kiril calls him.

"The break should be mended by now. Why is her arm still in the sling?" I whisper to Claude.

"Whatever is killing her is impairing her ability to heal."

Livia whimpers softly provoking Claude to move closer. Varian takes up the space next to me.

"She's so small." He looks perplexed.

"Children are like that." I respond.

"I've not been around a child in, I cannot recall the last time," he frowns.

"Vampires have kids, why haven't you seen any?"

"No parent desires to risk their offspring. What if I am as psychotic as people claim? Varian Caina, cursed with so much power he lost his sanity," he scoffs bitterly.

I plan to sneak off from him at his revelation. He's right. No one wants to chance being in his presence. Except maybe the doctor, whose qualifications I'm questioning now. Varian's hand grips my wrist like a vise.

"Relax, firefly. Gossip and superstition. You are safe with me."

"Could you loosen up on my wrist? I think I can feel the bones grinding."

Varian looks stricken. He holds my wrist up to inspect it for damage. Once he's satisfied I am unharmed, he lowers my hand down but refuses to let me go. His thumb rubs the backs of my fingers. Studying his features I take in the sharp angles of his face. The jaw, cheek, and nose are defined blades. His hair is blond, though not as light as my father's was. The Caina line is the height of vampire aristocracy. Varian possesses the looks to back his bloodline's claim. The length of his hair is his only rebellion from the polished features genetics granted him. It is long, past his shoulders. Vampires are beautiful. It makes them more efficient predators. Fae share that innate beauty in common with vampires. Varian Caina is the most attractive man I've ever seen in any realm.

Seriously? The most lethal Vampire in the entire world and I have a girl boner for him? I am so screwed.

"I think I would have liked to be a father." I can barely hear him he speaks so softly.

Squeezing his hand I say, "You still can. Not like you don't have lifetimes to do it." I meant for him to laugh at my joke.

He gives me a sad smile and my heart breaks for him. "I think you and I both know the score on that, firefly."

I start to say something to him, but I'm interrupted. The woman from Lune Rouge explodes into the bedroom with Bastien on her heels.

CHAPTER 16

Rachel

LIVIA LOOKS FRIGHTENING. Her skin is deathly pale; her lovely red hair has lost its shine. My heart is breaking in my chest. A man is bowed over her bed, surveying her then writing furiously in a notepad. He's not a Fae, I learned from meeting the Fae bartender, Winter, at Lune Rouge that they are mesmerizing. He doesn't hypnotize me with his beauty the way Winter does. No animal qualities, so not a shifter. He sticks his pen in between his teeth to turn the page on his notepad. Dangerously sharp canines, too long to be human, rest over the pen. Vampire. If I had not seen his teeth, I wouldn't have known.

So Arcana does have a point of weakness.

Crossing the room, I sit down in the chair next to Livia. I hold her uninjured hand in mine.

"Livia, its Rachel." Her eyes flutter but don't open. I glance over for Bastien, and find he's standing by my side. He seems torn between anger and sadness. His father Claude is close by. He mirrors his son's dark countenance.

"Livia, sweetheart, please wake up. I need to talk to you. I need to hear your voice. We're free. No more tests. No more bossy men in suits. You can be a little girl now." The tears fall fast. Livia blurs into a shape on the bed as my vision is clouded over with moisture. Bastien lifts me from the chair into his arms. With my face buried in his neck, I let myself sob. I cried until the tears ran out.

When I'm sure I've no moisture left in my body to give, I speak to Bastien. "You can put me down now. I think I am done."

He rumbles in his chest, and his arms get tighter. "I like you here."

I like me here, too.

"At least let me stand on my own two feet. Marriages are built on compromise."

"Human marriages maybe," He says as he sets me down.

I pause to take in the room's occupants. Claude has moved closer to Bastien and me. He catches me looking at him and supplies a nod. A simple greeting that feels full of favor. Winter has tear tracks down her cheek. One side of her face is pressed to the chest of a tall, handsome blond man. His arms are around her, and he's resting the side of his face on the top of her head.

Is that her husband?

The doctor closes his notepad and addresses the room. "Humans created a dangerous cocktail. Why did they infect the child?"

I clear my throat before I respond, "To use as leverage against me."

The doctor does not like that answer. He makes a scary face and says something in a language I don't understand. The blond man embracing Winter grunts in agreement.

"They call us monsters, yet they infect children with death." The Doctor sneers.

I jump like I was hit. Bastien rubs my arm to soothe me.

"Death? Does that mean you can't do anything for her?" Bastien asks before I can.

Mussing his hair, the doctor rubs at his head absently. "Our options are limited. Time is running out," he sighs. "With the samples I gathered I can give her a chance once I get the original compound they used. Magic would work, but the Fae refused the petition." The doctor wanders out of the room mumbling about cures, antigens, and blasted humans.

I find Winter's eyes and demand an answer. "I thought she was a Royal Red. Bastien said she was the daughter of some lost princess. Why won't they help?"

Winter disentangles herself from the stoic blond. Swiping at her eyes she says. "Because she's only half Fae. The queen will not help a halfling. If Amalia was alive, then she might be persuaded. Fae are not known for their loving families." Winter is angry for Livia. Guess not all Fae are anti-family.

Madalaina opens the door. "All of you look beat. Take a break. I am going to read to my niece for a bit, and I hate an audience."

I don't want to leave, but Bastien coaxes me out. There is nothing I can do here. The drive back to his place is quiet.

Our place, now.

Still hard for me to believe there *is* an us.

Will there always be an us? Are werewolves monogamous? All my stuff is still at my old apartment. Unless Anna got rid of it. This is making my head hurt.

We get back to the house and Bastien walks over to sit on one of the kitchen stools. His eyes aren't as bright as they usually are; dark circles have formed underneath them. Tension in his shoulders has him rubbing the back of his neck absentmindedly. I stop in front of him and replace his hands with mine. Gently massaging the knots drags a moan from him. He rests his forehead in the center of my chest. His arms hug me around the waist.

My poor wolf.

"What are we going to do, Bastien? If the Fae won't help, then we need to get back into Richland somehow and steal Keller a sample of the virus."

He grunts. "Is your plan to make me stupid with your sweet hands so I'll agree to anything? Because it's working."

In mock disbelief I ask, "Would I do something like that?"

Bastien pulls my arms down from his neck and slides his hands into mine. "I haven't known you long, but I would say without a doubt that you'd do anything to protect my niece."

I scoff at him calling Livia his niece.

Why am I mad? She is his niece.

Bastien pulls me onto his lap. "Why are you upset? I can feel you pulling away from me."

I duck my face. "It's stupid. I'm possessive of her and she isn't even related to me." I mumble.

Hugging me tighter, Bastien brushes my back with his hand. "She is now. You are her Aunt through our mate bond. But you two are so much more than that. You didn't give birth to

Livia, but you love her as fiercely as any mother. Blood doesn't always tie a family together."

"When this is all over will I lose her?" I whisper.

Tears again? I'm such a crybaby.

"No, baby. I won't let anyone take Livia from you. Once she's better she'll live here with us. First we have to get her well again. I think you're right about Richland. I'll get the sample for Keller."

I jump off Bastien's lap. "Are you crazy? Did you hear me at all when I told you what they do inside Richland? They could throw you in the tank with someone like me."

I'd be broken if he died. Whoa where did that come from? When did I fall in love so completely?

Angrily, I stalk out of the kitchen. I'm angry with myself for being vulnerable, angry with Richland for what he did to Livia and I am angry with Bastien for being so damn chivalrous.

Why'd he have to be such a great guy? This would be easier if he was a jerk.

A tingle in my hands signals to me that my Arcana is kicking into high gear along with my anger.

Bastien doesn't let me get far. He catches my hand and whirls me around to face him.

Ah! He needs to stop with all the alpha male manhandling! Maybe. Not really.

"Rachel, I'm sorry you're mad, but I won't let you go back there."

"Let me? How do you propose to stop me Mr. Macho?"

He smiles at me so seductively; I can feel myself

weakening.

Damn you traitorous girly bits.

"I think we both know I am a clever boy," he teases.

Who can stay mad at that? Hmph. He can think he's won for now. I won't stand by and watch him sacrifice his life for Livia and me. When I have the chance, I'm out of here. Keller will get his sample and Livia won't die. Not if I can help it.

CHAPTER 17

Bastien

I'M FURIOUS. Between lending emotional support to Rachel and trying to keep my anger under wraps, I'm stretched thin. My niece is dying.

I didn't know she existed until yesterday, and now she may not live past tomorrow.

My mate is in agony. It radiates off of her. When she broke down I wanted to rip something apart. I still do, but I need to focus on Rachel. She can't afford for me to go rogue.

Loving her is as effortless as breathing. After our talk I put her into bed. She needs the rest. I have too much pent up energy to sleep. I pace the living room. The change is sizzling within every fiber of my being. If I allow my wolf out, it will relax me, but up until now Rachel and I haven't talked about my furry side.

I don't want to freak her out on day two.

Shedding clothing usually helps. Stripped down to my jeans and bare feet I don't feel any better. Back to pacing, bouncing on the balls of my feet, rolling my shoulders, and ignoring the call to change.

I don't hear Rachel as she silently walks in. "Getting ready to box with someone?"

I shake my head.

I don't trust myself to speak without sounding like the big bad wolf.

My vocal cords are being affected by the need to shift.

Rachel ambles over and hooks a finger in my belt loop. "What can I do? Please don't shut me out."

I could expend some energy if I fucked her brains out.

Appealing as that sounds, I can't guarantee she wouldn't see me wolf out a little.

"Need to change." My voice is thick, which makes it hard to speak.

"Change? Into a wolf?"

I nod. She doesn't need to think about it before saying, "Okay. Am I safe if you change?"

"Always safe. With me." I struggle to get the words out.

"Then change. I'm not afraid."

This woman amazes me. Destiny has given me a mate I fear I am not worthy of. I'll worry about that later. Right now, I need release.

Rachel helps me remove my jeans. Her cheeks flush at my nudity. A born wolf, my transformation is quick and relatively painless. None of the popping and flesh tearing that bitten wolves endure. It used to be all of us were born wolves, now it is about fifty-fifty. An advantage to being a born wolf is I can choose the canine form or a human/wolf hybrid. The hybrid is similar to what you see in the horror movies. Made wolves only have the hybrid option. I decide to go for canine over horror movie to ease Rachel into it.

What woman wants to know they married The Howling?

The wolf takes over. My fur is white. It's rare and I'm proud of my coat.

She said she's okay, but no reason to throw her in the deep end without a life raft.

I give Rachel the chance to touch me. She hesitates, so I bump her thigh with my nose and whine. Tentatively, her fingers tunnel into my fur on the side of my neck. Gaining confidence she pets me and scratches my head.

Aw, damn. She hits a spot on my ear and my back leg starts kicking.

This is embarrassing. Yep, might as well neuter me now.

She giggles. "That good, huh? I think I have a few spots that make me jump too. You are welcome to explore them after you take a run."

A run, huh? I'll take a quick zip across my property. Won't take more than a few minutes, then I can explore those spots Rachel spoke of.

Mind made up I head for the side door. Rachel unlocks it, and I take off.

Wait, my wife just let me out like a dog.

Not how I envisioned life with a mate.

CHAPTER 18

Rachel

MY HUSBAND RUNS OFF to chase rabbits or whatever werewolves do. I can only shake my head and snicker. My life has detoured onto an unusual path. I put Bastien's jeans by the door so he can dress when he returns. The thought of prying eyes scrutinizing my gloriously naked man makes me twitch.

Possessive already. Opening yourself up for heartache, Rachel. What else can I do? Not claiming him for my own is laughable.

I hear the backdoor open and slam shut.

Home already? He just left!

I turn around. It's not Bastien. Miguel Lopez comes stalking into the room.

He shows up the minute Bastien leaves my side. Oh god, did he hurt Bastien?

I sprint for the bedroom, but he's faster. He picks me up and propels me across the living room into the wall cracking the plaster. My head is spinning as blood fills my mouth. Miguel pulls me up from the floor by my hair, and uses his body to crowd me.

Miguel's hand is around my throat, he applies pressure and leans in to whisper menacingly, "Hello, Bitch. We have unfinished business. Did you know the Lopez pack is the only full familial bitten pack? That means we're all made, not born. We're unique. The future. Better than those stuck up born assholes. Alonzo belonged to a legacy and you killed him."

I swallow around his hand. "I had no choice," I wheeze.

His fingernails are growing longer, sharp daggers digging into my neck. "You could have chosen to die instead."

Fat chance, Cujo. I like me a hell of a lot better than your legacy.

The edges of my vision are turning black. I am going to pass out and when I do I won't wake up ever again.

Where the hell is my Arcana?

I reach for it but my head throbs. I think Miguel gave me a concussion when he threw me into the wall and now it's seems to be out of reach.

"I'm not a monster, I'm not without mercy. I can be quick, kill you before you notice the pain."

Aren't you a gentleman?

Honestly, I pray he's telling the truth. I don't want to die. I want to live, build a life with Bastien. I want Livia to live, too. But I'm helpless. I can't fight anymore. I can feel my life slipping away.

Dear God, please, let the ones I love survive.

I open my eyes. Miguel looks hell bent on murdering me. We're nose to nose. In his pupils, I see my reflection. My ears register the wet crunch. Miguel's grasp loosens and precious oxygen fills my lungs. Miguel gurgles, blood streams out of his mouth. Between our bodies a red stain blooms across his shirt. His eyes release mine and turn to peer over his shoulder, behind him is Bastien.

A feral sneer curls his lips, and he growls, "I'm without

mercy."

Bastien moves away and allows Miguel's body to crumble to the ground. Carelessly, he drops something on top of him. It's Miguel's heart. Bastien pulled it out through his back.

I try to speak but a whimper tumbles out instead before darkness consumes me and I black out.

CHAPTER 19

Bastien

RACHEL IS SITTING on our bed. We just returned from the doctor. She has a concussion and a lot of bruising.

Miguel almost killed her with the force he used to throw her against the wall. It's a miracle she doesn't have any broken bones.

A bruise in the shape of Miguel's hand is visible on her throat. There are lacerations where he cut her with his claws. My father sent a cleaning crew over to take care of the mess while I accompanied Rachel to the hospital. When we returned the body was gone, the carpet showed no trace of blood, and the plaster was repaired. Gone for two hours, and the house looks normal again. Werewolves are notoriously violent, makes sense we know how to clean up a mess.

I haven't spoken since it happened. Holding back, but I can't anymore. "How dare he touch you? I'll collect the head of every member of his clan, starting with his mother. If my father won't support me, I'll challenge him for the pack. No one will touch you without fear their entire house will be wiped out."

"Bastien, you can't do that,"

"I'm the alpha! I can do what I damn well please!"

What the hell? I'm not the alpha.

I'm seething, and Rachel is grinning at me. She's pissing me off. Rachel crawls towards the edge of the bed. All she's wearing is one of my shirts and her panties. Perched on her knees she crooks a finger at me to come closer. I come near enough for her to unbutton my jeans.

I mildly attempt to dissuade her. "Rachel, you're injured, and I'm so angry I might combust."

"I feel stronger. My head doesn't hurt and my back feels great. Even my throat seems to have recovered."

I tip her jaw back to carefully inspect.

Well I'll be damned.

She's right. Her bruises are fading. Fading too fast. The advanced healing is a benefit from our mating or something they did to her at Richland.

Either way, I'm glad.

"Still in no shape for sex, Love."

Rachel won't let me tell her no. "Bastien, I'm alive. I was certain I was dying. I imagined I'd never see you again. Instead, I'm breathing and whole with my sexy mate. I. Want. You." Her fingernails score my abs under my shirt. Her lips caress my neck.

"Rachel, I can't be gentle right now. I'm begging you to stop," I plead.

"Then don't be gentle," She whispers in my ear.

That's all I can take. I grip the bottom of her shirt and tear it from her. I shoulder her backward and follow her down, spreading kisses on her breasts. Rachel's hands are everywhere, my back, my neck, my scalp. She pouts when I untangle myself from her hands and sit up. I look at her flushed skin and the marks on her breasts left by me. I like seeing them. My lust boils over, and it gets worse when she runs her hands over her breasts, down her abdomen and into her underwear. I halt her hand. I'm graced with another one of those pretty pouts. She gasps when I grip her underwear and shred them.

Hope she didn't like that pair.

"I knew you were mine from the start. The way you smell makes me crazy." I bury my face between her thighs. I want to make her scream my name. At the first touch of my tongue, she moans. Fingers burrow through my hair. I continue to lick as I slip two fingers inside. Turning them up I search for the g-spot. Now that I am working them both Rachel is rocking against my face.

"Oh my god, Bastien! Don't stop, please don't stop!" She begs. Her moaning turns to cries.

The orgasm ripples through her as she screams and bucks her hips. I use my free hand to prevent her from getting free. I maintain my onslaught until she screams my name a second time. Rachel has a minute to recover while I finish getting my jeans off. Naked, I slide up Rachel's body. Hitching her right leg up over my hip, I line myself up and roughly slide into heaven. She cries out and orders me to do it again. Gripping her hips tight, I roll us over so she's riding me.

The switch doesn't faze her. She finds her rhythm rocking above me. Her hands find their way to her breasts. Massaging them, she rolls her nipples between her fingertips. Rachel rotates her hips, and I think I see stars. I bring my hand down between us and use my thumb to bring her to another orgasm;

she splinters in my arms. Her hands thrust up into her hair, and she throws her head back. A few thrusts and I find my own release. Rachel collapses on my chest panting. All my anger is gone, replaced by a gratefulness that I am still able hold her.

CHAPTER 20

July 7

Rachel

BASTIEN IS ASLEEP. After today's trauma and the great sex we just had; I don't see him waking anytime soon. My heart constricts.

How am I going to leave this man?

If all goes according to plan, I'll be fine.

Chances are I'm not going to be fine.

I must go back to The Richland Institute. Livia needs the antidote if she's going to survive. Keller needs the virus to make the cure. I won't let Bastien go there. I slip out of bed and get dressed. After I write Bastien a note, I leave.

I'm jittery. Whatever those hacks injected me with is getting stronger. I'm scared.

What if the Arcana gets too intense and I can't manage it?

A buzzing of electricity runs in my veins. I'm a live wire. My emotions are tied to the Arcana. Richland wanted me to become a weapon. Well, he's going to witness first hand if his project is a success or a failure.

I walk up to the front door of The Richland Institute like I own it. The building appears innocuous from the outside.

The windows with bars must face a different side.

I barely step one foot inside the front door when people start screaming at me to lie on the floor. I comply, and a guard sticks a knee in my back to hold me down while a nurse injects me with something.

Already with the needles and drugs?

I don't know how long I was out for. I wake up groggy. My mouth tastes thick with cotton. Lying perfectly still, I close my eyes and use my power to assess the situation. I can sense the guards. There are a lot of them. Dr. Morris is in the room next door. He's arguing with someone over my brain scans.

Ah, there's Richland.

Dr. Morris is giving him a progress report.

"Her readings are phenomenal. I dared not dream this level of psychic ability was possible from the virus."

"I understand Dr. Morris, but if I can't witness a demonstration for myself I won't accept the readings as anything more than scratches on paper."

"Well, yes sir, I agree. We should examine her abilities, but if Gates' death taught us anything, it's she can't be forced to perform."

Richland laughs at him. They're getting closer.

Time to get this show on the road.

The curtain around my bed is pulled back.

Richland is smirking at me. "Good evening Miss Ryan. May we speak?" Ever the coward, guards flank both sides of him as he approaches me.

Afraid of something?

"You can go to hell." I reply sweetly.

The bastard chuckles and steps closer. I cannot stress how hard I am holding myself back from killing this man where he stands. His orders condemned Livia to death.

"You will go back into the testing tank. I desire to see what new tricks you have learned."

I want to scream. I'm terrified to go in there again. I think I can defend myself, but maybe I just got lucky before. After all I couldn't fight Miguel off. How do I know I will be able to face whoever they decide to pit against me?

Richland wants to watch me kill someone, someone who may be just like me.

That leaves a sour taste in my mouth.

"We will be back for you at eight in the morning. Be ready."

Richland walks out leaving the door open. Searching the walls for a clock, I discover I only have four hours. Dr. Morris remains next to the bed.

"Something I can help you with, Doc?" I ask him.

He refuses eye contact. "The girl. Livia. Is she dead?"

"Not yet. Soon," I grit out.

He rubs the back of his neck and sighs, "You have every right to hate me. I am not a nice man. My experiments have destroyed thousands of lives, for which I am sure I will be severely punished for one day. But I want you to know I cared for Livia. I delivered her. Her mother loved her even with the forced conception. She died before naming her. I looked at the baby, and I was changed. I named her. I tried to protect her. In the end, I failed."

Dr. Morris left me behind in shock. I still hate the man, but a miniscule piece of me can empathize with him.

A microscopic itty-bitty part of me. I won't cry when he dies.

High heels clicking on the linoleum signal the arrival of another person in the room, but I can't see them. The stranger speaks to Morris and I hear a voice I thought I'd never hear again. Anna, my ex-roommate, has come calling.

I guess that answers the question of whether or not she was in on the scheme to kidnap me.

Sugary sweet, Anna asks Morris to leave us alone. "Girl talk, you know? We have some catching up to do."

Looking at Anna, she doesn't appear as perfect as I once thought she was. She's high maintenance with salon styled hair, perfect manicure, and designer clothes. In this light she is more of a manufactured beauty not a natural.

Perfect Anna, a perfect bitch.

Scowling at her, I caution, "Do you really want to be alone with me, Anna? You fall third on the list of people I want to see slowly disemboweled."

She snorts and crosses her arms over her chest. "You are tied to the bed, what can you do to me?"

You have no idea, honey.

As much as I hate to admit it, seeing Anna hurts. Her presence confirms that she was never my friend, knowing this now, I can't feel happy she's okay.

Does it make me a bad person that I hoped she was genuine and died because of it?

"Tell me why, Anna. I want to know what was in it for you, were we ever friends at all?"

She throws her head back and laughs, "This was never about being your friend, Rachel, there's so much more at stake here."

My turn to chuckle. "You expect me to believe you're on Richland's genocide bandwagon? No offense sweetie, but you were never the brightest bulb in the box, I have a hard time thinking of you as a criminal mastermind."

Anna narrows her eyes at me. "I don't know what genocide means, but I'm not stupid."

Debatable.

Frustrated and ready for this conversation to be over I growl at Anna to tell me why.

"Stu tells me who the targets are and I get them for a price. My Stu Bear is very generous when I'm a good girl,"

"Oh gag me. You *sleep* with Richland? That's almost as bad as your role in kidnapping people for his sick experiments. Almost. And why do you do it? For spa days and expensive handbags. I think it's time for you to go, Anna."

My tolerance cup runneth over with bullshit.

A nasty snarl curls Anna's lips, "I'll leave when I'm ready. You can't make me do anything in your position." She sounds smug and satisfied with herself.

I stop paying attention, but it doesn't stop Anna from continuing with a litany of cruel comments.

Why won't she shut up?

Her tirade shows no signs of being over anytime soon,

and I can't stand to listen to her voice a second longer.

"Last warning, Anna. Get lost," I say through clenched teeth.

Anna ignores me, unfortunately for her. Unleashing my fury fueled Arcana, I 'grab' her jaw and wrench it to the side until it breaks. The grotesque angle it rests at is horrible to look at. She's freaking out, trying to scream but it's garbled. Anna crowds her hands near her face but doesn't touch her jaw.

Innocently, I say, "Wow, Anna, something's wrong with your jaw. You should probably have that looked at."

Anna stumbles backward frightened and trips in her heels. She lands on her ass, jarring her broken jaw so that it flaps.

That's just not right.

Dr. Morris trots back in to see what all the commotion is about. His eyes bug out when he sees Anna. He tries to help her up, but she slaps his hands away. Back on her feet, Anna runs out the door.

Morris looks at me bewildered. "What happened to her?"

I pin him with a hard stare, "Looks like she suffered an unfortunate accident."

Morris sputters and retreats from the exam room leaving me alone.

It's possible Anna will go running to Richland to tattle, but I'd bet she's too vain to let him see her in a mangled state.

I could just grab vials from the storage fridge and run, but I have to finish what I started here. I don't think I can move on until I do this. The next few hours crawl by. Richland is true to his word. At eight o'clock sharp, two orderlies and six armed soldiers come to fetch me. When we reach the tank, I hesitate. Whatever is in there it's going to be terrible. I can't help Livia if I don't do this. I stand a little straighter and proceed inside. Two men follow us carrying a body bag. They place it in the center of the room. All Richland personnel exit quickly.

I try not to think about what or who is inside the bag, but curiosity gets the better of me. Carefully I unzip the top and peer in. The occupant is no stranger to me. Alonzo and his wolf lay inside. He has begun to decay. I choke back the vomit rising in my throat. The smell makes me gag and hold my nose. They'd crudely sewn the two together.

However they plan to reanimate him I doubt he'll be happy to see me.

The lights in the viewing room turn on. The Armani squad files into the room with Richland; Dr. Morris is absent.

My audience has arrived.

I see the men sitting on one side of the room, practically on top of each other. The reason they bunch together walks in last. Kadema Sidell, the voodoo king.

I agree with the suits. The man is freaking scary.

Kadema must be here to raise Alonzo from the dead.

Yippee Skippy.

"Alright, gentlemen. Let's see what your funding has purchased." Richland points at Kadema. "Raise the beast and make it attack. Miss Ryan, I suggest you fight back."

I flip him the bird. Kadema is chanting. Alonzo is twitching.

Shit, shit, shit.

CHAPTER 21

Winter

SNEAKING INTO FAIRY is the dumbest idea I've ever had. It's hard to do without the right connections. Lucky me I know a few kind hearts in the Unseelie Court willing to sneak me in just to stick it to the Seelie Fae. Ianthe isn't a bad person, truth be told she's a bit odd for a Siren. She's very sweet and not in the 'I'm waiting to seduce you and kill you' way. I'd be an idiot to trust any Siren though.

The portal isn't meant for mortals. Without my magic intact, it makes me dizzy to travel back and forth across the planes. I'm not alone, Varian is with me. He won't leave.

I have my very own vampire stalker.

We're here to meet Kiril. He stole back my magic to heal Livia. She will not last long enough for the Tribunal to decide a plan of action against The Richland Institute. They'll do what is beneficial for all the races, not just one sick child caught in the middle.

I can do something though. I won't allow her to die.

"This is fun." Varian is grinning ear to ear.

"You need to get out more," I mutter.

"I try, but there is all the yelling and terror. It grates on my nerves. People get hurt when I become annoyed. Better for everyone if I remain a hermit."

Good lord, this man is demented.

Kiril isn't at the spot we agreed upon, but he left me a present. My magic. Taking magic out hurts because your body feels lost. Putting magic back in is a whole other level of pain because you're shoving a lot of energy into a flesh and blood vessel. Magic is inert without a body to wield it, and as a royal, we have some seriously powerful enchantments running through our bloodline.

Suck it up, Winter. Time to get your mojo back.

The smooth moonstone inside of the box is cold in my hands. I lovingly lift it from the box and hold it over my heart. The heat begins to build from the contact. Flames lick my skin covering every inch of my body.

I can't take anymore.

Varian snatches my free hand.

Panicking. I ask him, "What are you doing? You will kill yourself!"

He won't let go. His eyes are hard. The pain ebbs. "Just taking the edge off, firefly."

When I fully absorb the power I feel alive.

I missed this.

Varian is a little ruffled, but otherwise okay. He isn't burnt to a crisp like I feared.

"Wow, firefly. You were beautiful before, but with magic you are breathtaking." He whispers awestruck.

The Queen's guard interrupts us. Dressed in scarlet and gold, they surround us. Varian tenses, but I put a hand on his forearm. These men are following orders. I'll take the fight where it belongs.

"Halt, By order of the Queen! Winter Summersun you are in violation of exile. Trespassing in Fairy is punishable by death."

The Queen's guard transports us to the castle immediately. It's not a long walk so I have limited time to figure out a plan. My Grandmother sits atop her throne. The whole Court has turned out for this showdown.

How does word travel so fast in the Fae plane?

"Winter. Why are you trespassing?" She demands. Her eyes narrow on me and she gasps, "Who gave you back your magic?"

"No one gave it to me I took it."

"Impossible," she scoffs. "You couldn't have acted alone."

"She isn't alone," says Varian stepping forward.

"A vampire? Are you the junkyard dog doing her bidding?" Tanith sneers.

Varian's eyes flash. "I am Lord Varian Caina of the House of Caina. I am no dog. If you are suggesting I willingly do Winter's dirty work, then yes." His air of authority is intimidating.

Tanith pales. The Court shrinks back. Varian Caina's reputation is known far and wide. Aware of her audience, Tanith recovers her composure. "It doesn't matter. Winter is subject to the Fae Court. She must pay for her crimes."

My turn to be the bitch.

"You will let us leave peacefully or I will reveal what I read in the Book of Dawns." My trump card is played.

Tanith's grip on her throne tightens, cracking the delicate wood.

For an old biddy she's strong.

Her eyes narrow at me and she grinds her teeth. "Take your vampire and go. Just know this isn't finished, Winter." She warns me.

"It had better be Tanith." Varian counsels her. "If anything happens to Winter, I will come for you. I read the book, Tanith. I know. After I tell everyone the truth you'll die screaming a slow death." Varian grasps my arm, and in a blink we're back at his house.

Holy crap! How did he do that? Varian can teleport?

"You never said you could teleport in and out of Fairy!" I accuse.

He smiles in return. "You never asked."

Infuriating ass.

"You told Tanith you know what is in the Book of Dawns. Was that a lie, Varian? I was given the impression that only a handful of Fae and your doctor know the truth."

Did he read the book when I wasn't paying attention or did he already know?

"I've no idea what is in that damned book. I bluffed. Might be a good idea to tell me since I lied to leverage your continued safety." Arms crossed over his chest Varian waits for me to tell him.

"It's too dangerous. It's better if you don't know."

"Winter. Tell me. If you don't tell me then I will be forced to torture Keller until he tells me. Do you want that on your conscience?"

"Fine. Fae and vampires are mortal enemies. None of us know why. According to the book, we're the same species. Vampires were a race of Unseelie dark Fae before the Courts split into Summer and Winter. One day, the queen at the time banished them for no reason. Both sides refuse to acknowledge the connection. After a while, the truth disappeared with its descendants. The Book of Dawns is the only record."

"You're telling me I'm a fairy?" His gaze is incredulous.

"Yep. You're a fairy."

Shaking his head he says, "Embarrassing. Don't fret, I won't be sharing that news anytime soon. Let's go save the girl."

CHAPTER 22

Bastien

RACHEL IS GONE. She left a note. A damn note. She's got this crazy idea she is the only one who can save Livia. She's going back to The Richland Institute to get a sample for the vampire doctor.

How does she plan to get back out of that place?

I won't be sitting around to find out. The Tribunal is meeting right now, and I'm going to crash it.

The Therian Council is present. Manias Artorias, the Vampire Regis, and a representative for the witches attended, but there are no Fae in sight.

Figures.

Uptight bunch never did care about the trials we face as a species, since they don't live on the human plane.

My father sees me and stands up from the table. "Bastien, what's happened?"

"Rachel. She's gone. She went back to The Richland Institute to try and save Livia." I silently plead with him to help me get my mate back.

He sighs and sits back down. "Bastien, I'm sorry. There is nothing I can do."

I shout, "Yes there is! You're the alpha. You can lead us into war. A war we're already a part of. Our people are being tortured and tested inside that place. They have my mate. I intend to end this!"

There is sympathy in his eyes but stone in his voice, my father doesn't like being ordered to act. "You're right, I *am* the alpha. I'm not convinced war is the correct path."

Speaking loud enough for all to hear I announce, "Then I challenge for the position of alpha."

The room erupts into chaos. Everyone arguing and taking sides. Regis Manias slams his fist down on the table, cracking the wood.

"Everyone shut up! A challenge has been issued. It has to be met." Manias makes the declaration and slips back into the quiet calm that he's notorious for.

Cleary Neil, a lion shifter, leans forward in his chair. "I will support Bastien's claim for alpha."

Jay, the massive grizzly therian next to him, nods his approval of my claim. Two supporters are all I need to move forward with my challenge.

Dad stands up again and meets me toe to toe. "Dad, you have to step down or fight me. I don't want to kill you."

Please, don't make me do this.

My restraint is slipping. Every second we sit and debate is another that Rachel needs me.

I have no time for this political bullshit.

Dad reaches out a hand and places it on my shoulder. "I've felt the shift in you since the girl arrived. I knew she would bring the alpha in you to the surface. You're strong,

Bastien. You always have been. You never cared for power or rank before, but now you have someone to protect. If I fight you, I know I can hold my own. I would leave you with an injury that plagues you until the end of your days. Make you vulnerable to other attacks. But in the end, I won't be able to win. I refuse to leave my son in a weakened state to rule. I step down as Alpha Prime and recognize our new leader, Sebastien Bonvillian."

Dad sinks to his knees in front of me; head down and neck exposed. The other shifters have to follow suit or it's considered a challenge. Everyone complies. Cleary has a shit-eating grin on his face that's borderline insolence.

The poor witch representing the Covens, I think she's going to throw up.

Probably not used to all the commotion that comes with the therian society.

"That's settled. As Regis I recognize you as the Alpha Prime on behalf of the vampires. A good choice," says Manias.

The Regis is a powerful ally.

I could use a man like him in my corner.

"Will you fight with us?"

"Publicly? Of course not. Coincidentally, I've a few guards with a little free time that might want to stretch their legs. What do you say, Nikolai?"

I hadn't even noticed him. The man stepped out of the shadows behind the king's chair.

Nikolai, I've heard his name before.

The guard he leads is the highest order of vampire

warriors. They're called Wraiths, this is because they don't even exist. Ghosts. An outsider would assume Manias goes everywhere unguarded. He'd be wrong. It is estimated that twenty Wraiths accompany the Regis at all times.

How do you hide twenty assassins in one room?

It might sound far-fetched, but I was not eager to test it for truth.

Nikolai stands poised for action at Manias' side. "Rescue a damsel in distress from a fortress filled with humans who like to torture people? I think we're free for that. How many men will you be taking in, Alpha?"

"I'll call in the ranks, take the strongest without depleting our defense here." Doing a little mental math I say, "Around two hundred."

"Two hundred and one," amends Cleary.

"Two," grumbles Jay.

The witch, Seraphina, raises her hand to get my attention. She clears her throat and swallows nervously before speaking. "We can supply you with some charms, and spells to make any of the innocent people inside of the institute fall asleep."

Witches. Always siding with the humans. What makes her think there are any innocent people?

"It isn't much, but the charms will protect you," she continues. "The sleeping spell will make it easier to spot targets."

Better than nothing, I guess.

I nod at her. "I won't turn it down."

I hear Nikolai's faint Russian accent. "Two hundred and two shifters, along with some witchy hocus pocus, and my

Wraiths. I should need, say five Wraiths. That should be enough."

Manias chuckles. "Five Wraiths are a bit over kill don't you think?

The soldier grins hugely. "Yes, Regis, but it will be a spectacular battle."

CHAPTER 23

Varian

CLAUDE'S HOUSE IS IN CHAOS. People are armed to the teeth. Shifters of all varieties are gearing for battle.

Must have missed a memo while I was out playing thief with Winter.

I spy snakes, random cats, a huge bear, a lion, and a shit load of wolves. Five vampires in black fatigues are sitting off to the side looking bored.

Wait, are those Wraiths?

"Nikolai?"

His buzzed blond head pops up. "Varian! What are you doing here? Come to join us?"

I wave him off. "Nah, following a fairy. She's been pretty entertaining. I threatened the Queen of the Fae. Again." I grin unrepentantly.

Nikolai pulls me aside. He looks serious.

He's always so serious.

"Don't start any wars, Varian. Manias has enough to deal with." He points over to Manias deep in conversation with Bastien.

"I make no promises." Backing away with my hands up in playful surrender, I catch Winter heading up the staircase to

Livia, so I jog to catch up.

"Do you think your magic will be enough to save her?"

"God, I hope so."

I enter the room and see Livia is wearing an oxygen mask. Her heart rate is dangerously slow. Madalaina is sitting beside her.

Winter must be friends with her.

She walks over and hugs the werewolf. Keller is seated at a desk across the room writing in one of his damn notebooks. There are thousands of them in my house filled with his chicken scratch.

I jostle the man making him mess up whatever he was writing. "Keller. We brought Fae magic. Winter can help her."

He huffs at me, before standing up and walking over to the bed.

I do enjoy irritating that man. Not his fault they made him my keeper.

Winter shifts closer to the child. She lays her palms on Livia's broken body. She places one on her feverish brow, and one over her weakening heart. Slowly building in intensity, a golden light glows all around Livia. Winter's magic is strong, but I can see it's not strong enough. Covering her hands with my own, I boost her magic. Her skin feels warm and comforting, the healing enchantment is strengthened with the addition of my own magic. Together we push the crude man made sickness out of Livia. The child begins to convulse, coughing and gagging. Madalaina helps Livia lean over the bed to vomit into a trashcan. Viscous black slime forcefully expels out of her mouth. She chokes a few times, but Keller pats her back to help dislodge the blockage. After what feels like an eternity, the vomiting stops.

Keller helps Livia lay back against the pillows. Madalaina retrieves a damp cloth to clean her face. The machine monitoring her heart is registering a regular beat and her skin holds a healthy pallor once again. Livia is only barely conscious, she keeps asking for Rachel. Madalaina begins to cry tears of joy. *We did it. We saved her.*

"All of you need to move so I can check my patient."

Keller gives the little girl a clean bill of health. Even her broken wrist is healed. My chest feels tight with emotion. I can't help myself; I pull Winter out of the room.

Across the hall is another bedroom. I gently push her into the bedroom and close the door behind us. Winter looks mad about the rough treatment, but I cut her off before she can complain.

"Come home with me." I play with a strand of her lavender hair to avoid her eyes.

"And do what?" she asks softly.

Exasperated, I throw my hands up and shake my head. "Talk, watch a movie, play board games, I don't care. Just be with me."

Winter doesn't get a chance to answer. A dark haired Fae man burst into the room out of breath.

Winter hurries to him and worriedly looks him over. "Kiril? What are you doing here?"

Who the fuck is he? Should I kill him? Winter is mine, damn it.

Kiril struggles to catch his breath. "Running. If they find

me, they'll kill me."

Winter looks at me and back at Kiril. "If who catches you?"

"The Queen's guard. She knows I helped you. I need your help, Winter."

This is about to throw a wrench in my plans.

Winter stares at me, and I know I've lost her.

Barely mine and already she's being taken from me. Life is ridiculously unfair.

Winter reaches out a hand to touch me. "I'm sorry, Varian. I should go."

I cannot meet her gaze. I recoil from her grasp and leave.

CHAPTER 24

Rachel

I SMOOTH MY HAND over the glass between the Armani squad and me.

Sturdy enough to stop a train. Can it hold a scared, psychically enhanced woman? Let's find out.

I count the occupants of the viewing room. Six suits plus Richland and Kadema.

No guards? I'm insulted.

They look nervous with me watching them so closely. Surely they wonder why I am not concerning myself with the zombie wolf in the body bag.

Priorities, boys.

I concentrate on the men in the viewing room. Invisible hands wrapped around their greedy throats.

Can't allow anyone to call for help.

The electric tingle under my skin amplifies. Blue ribbons of energy surge around me. Directing it through the glass and into the room with the men, it curls around their necks like a lover before pulling tightly. Multiple cracks fill the silence. The viewing window shatters.

Kadema has stopped chanting, the body bag stills. Richland trips over a chair to get out the door.

Damn, missed him.

I missed Kadema as well; guards will be swarming any minute.

"Most impressive." Kadema applauds me.

Not the reaction I expected but I'll accept it.

"I just want to leave. If you don't attack me, then I won't attack you."

"I've no desire to test who is stronger. Perhaps another time." He exits the room.

Perhaps you can go screw yourself buddy.

The tank door is locked, but since I shattered the glass barrier to the viewing window with my Arcana I can crawl through it and out of the tank. The popping of gunfire nearby indicates guards are close. I find myself slipping on my rush out of the viewing room. My whole left side is covered in blood; I look over Kadema's lifeless eyes are staring up at me. Somehow Kadema was gunned down. The warmth reaches my skin and I shudder in disgust.

A soldier yells to the others, "Hold your fire! Orders are to take the subject alive."

Nope. I will die fighting or leave with the virus. There will be no more experiments or tests.

"I don't want to hurt you. Get out of my way," I snarl.

"Get down on the floor!"

I tried to be nice.

All at once, I break the wrists and fingers of the four soldiers pointing guns at me. Can't pull the trigger if your hands are worthless. I start to feel sorry for them; they're just following orders.

You know what? Forget that!

They still recognize what is right and what is wrong.

I let them live. That's more generous than Richland.

The institute has most likely caused countless deaths.

I make it down a few corridors before I encounter guards again. Nurses and random personnel see me but don't approach.

I am drenched in blood, after all.

Bizarrely, I find employee after employee passed out, sleeping like babies, each and every one. Stepping around them, I count my blessings.

If they're unconscious, I don't have to deal with them.

Finding the lab is easy, thanks to the maps posted on every wall. Dr. Morris is lying on an exam table with his hand behind his head.

"I wondered when you would get here," he says.

I'm developing an eye twitch from dealing with these people.

"Been waiting for me long?"

He's staring at the ceiling. "I figured if you got free, you would want revenge."

I snort. "Shows what you know. I don't want revenge. I want Livia healed. I can't do that without the virus you injected into her."

Sitting up on the table, Morris finally looks at me. "You are a better person than me."

"Toxic waste is better than you. Can we quit the chit-chat? I need the virus, now!"

I expect him to argue but he hops off the table and goes to

the storage fridge. Morris retrieves vials and stuffs handfuls of them into a cooler bag.

"Take these to whoever is helping you on the outside. They're the most utilized in the lab. Follow me. I can take you down a back hall. Won't get you all the way out of the building, but you can bypass some of the guards."

I'm hesitant to follow him, but my options are limited. I strap the bag full of vials across my back.

The hallway is deserted. We arrive at a guard cage that separates the employee corridor from the main halls. Morris unlocks the gate for me using his key card. The old guy inside the guard cage is asleep. Security monitors line one wall; soldiers on every screen stalk me.

"I can slow them down," says Morris.

He logs into the computer terminal. I watch the security monitors. Morris electronically opens all the cells.

Uh…not sure that was wise.

The shit hits the fan immediately. I doubt every prisoner in the cells is dangerous. Some of them are bound to be weak or a non-aggressive species. Judging by the carnage on the screen, those that can fight are more than making up for those that can't. Time to go while the chaos ensues.

"Maybe you should stay here, in the cage," I say to Morris. "Any one of those prisoners is probably just itching to kill you."

"I appreciate the concern, but I can't live with what I've done any longer. I want to die." He looks down and fat crocodile tears splash the floor.

I have to roll my eyes. Morris is being melodramatic. He doesn't really want to die. He feels guilt and he should, but I don't buy that he's suddenly sorry.

He's sorry he got caught.

A blast rocks the building. Morris and I rush back to the monitors. Through the dust and rubble, we observe shifters headed into the building through a huge hole. They blew out the side of the lobby. Werewolves make up the majority of the mob. A large white wolf leads them.

My knight in shining armor, err...shaggy fur rides again.

"What's happening?" Morris asks me.

Grinning at the monitors, I shake my head.

I should have figured he'd make a grand entrance.

"I think my husband has come to fetch me."

There's a scuffling sound overhead. Ceiling tiles fall revealing black clad commandos. They drop down surrounding us. Not waiting for them to give an introduction I blast Arcana at them, propelling them back up into the ceiling and through the floor above.

Sayonara.

Morris is long gone when I turn around.

He's on his own.

I take off running towards the front entrance. I only need to make it as far as Bastien. I'm jumping over bodies and dodging the fight. The hole Bastien made is less than a hundred feet in front of me. I shouldn't have stopped to catch my breath. Someone grabs me by my hair. They're dragging me back as I scream Bastien's

CHAPTER 25

Bastien

THE SHIFTERS DESCEND on The Richland Institute like a plague. Nikolai and his Wraiths are somewhere. He didn't like my plan to use explosives. Too loud. Said he'd find a way in that didn't alert the world to our presence.

Inside the building, humans are fighting for their lives. Shifters I don't recognize, vampires, dark Fae, and creatures I've never seen before are attacking guards.

Did Rachel do all this?

I find myself proud of her. Cleary and Jay are rounding up unarmed civilians. They're awake which implies they're guilty of crimes against us, but we won't kill them until we know the extent of their involvement. It wasn't a popular order, but I like to believe we are better than the animals running this place. Manias has something up his sleeve and I'm playing along. Not all of them deserve to die. A man tries to resist Jay, big mistake there. He takes a grizzly paw to the face. Cleary is lying on another uncooperative man. The guy is struggling to get free, but with a bored looking lion on top of him, he doesn't stand a chance.

Cleary and Jay's idea of crowd control; sit on them. Lazy bastards.

A woman's shrill scream breaks my train of thought.

"Bastien!"

Rachel screams for me. A geezer in a suit has his hands on her. She's covered in blood.

Not a drop of it better belong to her.

In my wolf form, I can smell her fear. I snarl, sprinting towards her.

The old man viciously yanks Rachel's head back. "Stop! Or I'll shoot her." He yells at me.

Skidding to a halt, I growl quietly. Slowly circling him I look for weak spots.

"Richland, it's over. Give up," Rachel says.

"Shut your whore mouth!" He pulls her hair again. "I give you the power to go beyond mere mortal limitations, and you choose to fornicate with animals? You are worse than they are."

Richland is so focused on his tirade and me; he doesn't realize death stalks him from behind. The werewolf is abnormally large. His shift is wrong, something they did to him here no doubt. Matted hair hangs down his back and a mass of dark shag obscures his face. On his right pectoral is the tattoo #634860. He hones in on the man holding my mate. The hatred rolls off him. He doesn't care if my mate is hurt in the crossfire. I must be fast. Dipping low I prepare to pounce. Claws extended, #634860 grips his prey by the back of the neck. I leap, knocking Rachel to the floor. The smell of gunpowder permeates the air.

CHAPTER 26

#634860

I WAS READY when the doors to my cell opened. I kept myself alert for any opportunity. Time ceased for me the day I was taken. With no way to track the days, I don't know how many years have passed. The doctor, Morris is his name, cut me open too many times to count. Injections did god-awful things to me. My wolf is a mutated monster. I barely recognize myself anymore.

The worst thing they ever did was force the Fae woman on me. Morris gave me pills that drove me into a mating frenzy. They shoved her in my cell. She was beautiful, not that it would matter with the drugs in my system. I swear I did everything in my power to be careful and not hurt her. She didn't fight me, just cried.

I should've fought harder.

Morris told me she died delivering our child, a girl. I was horrified. A child? What will they do to her? What do they want with her? If I ever meet her, how can I look at her without hating myself? I don't know if the girl still lives, but I'll find out, make sure she's safe.

First, I want blood. I want Richland. This sick and twisted man orchestrates everything that goes on in this place. I cut a bloody swath through the guards. Richland is attempting to flee when I find him.

I figured the first place he would try for was the door.

He's holding a woman hostage, a gun at her side. I can't get him and ensure the woman is not harmed.

Collateral damage. She's not my problem.

I seize Richland by the neck. My claws sink in deep enough I touch his spine. He fires his gun, shooting me in the gut. I swat the gun away like a child's toy. The wound hurts like hell, but I will heal eventually.

"Hello, Richland. Been a long time." I squeeze tighter.

Terror dilates Richland's eyes. "Let me go, please."

Tilting my head to the side and frowning I repeat, "Please? How many times has someone said the same to you?"

Adding my other hand around his throat, I shake him. His head pops off his shoulders.

The woman gasps. I forgot about the hostage. She's on the floor with her mate who is now in human form beside her.

Narrowing my eyes at him I ask "Bastien?"

CHAPTER 27

Rachel

THE PSYCHO WOLF *knows my husband. Wonderful.*

I have more pressing matters to think about—Livia.

"Bastien, we should go. The virus, Keller can make a cure for Livia."

Bastien cannot drag his eyes off psycho wolf. He stands up, pulling me to my feet with him. Bastien is naked as a jaybird. I grab a lab coat off a chair nearby and thrust it at him.

"After you left, Winter came back with Fae magic." Bastien puts the lab coat on. "Livia was sitting up, and talking when I left."

I throw myself in his arms. I am relieved.

Is it all over?

Bastien's hug is not overly enthusiastic. He sets me aside. Slowly he moves towards the stranger.

"Athan? Is it really you?" Bastien asks Psycho.

"What's left of me? I am not the brother you remember," he replies.

He reaches out a hand to Athan. "You're still my brother. That's all that matters."

Athan recoils. A mixture of horror, anger, and distrust fall over his face. "No, it isn't. I am sorry Bastien, this cannot be a family reunion."

So this is Livia's father, Bastien and Madalaina's brother. Better stop calling him Psycho.

I hate to ask him, but I must. My stomach burns with fear and resentment.

"You have a daughter. She's beautiful, kind. She deserves a family after all she's been through. What will you do with her?" I ask him bitterly.

He doesn't answer, just carefully assess me before walking away. Bastien's heart is breaking. His pain throbs in my chest.

Psychic energy or mate bond, whatever the cause, it sucks to feel your lover's anguish.

Police sirens scream and flashing lights bounce off the concrete walls through the hole in the building.

Tugging on his hand I urgently say, "Bastien, the cops are here."

"It's taken care of. Come on." Disappointment and the adrenaline let down from the battle are making us both weary.

The fighting stopped. All the bad guys are either dead or in custody. The innocent are waking up. Witches guide them to exits under an enchantment. They leave without noticing the carnage.

Lucky bastards. Magical blinders.

I recognize familiar faces outside. Shifters from the Tribunal stand next to a podium.

What the hell is a podium doing out front?

Whoa! Press and news crews are swarming. Human police are intercepting the captives and handcuffing them. A vampire takes the podium. "Ladies and Gentlemen of the press, good evening. My name is Manias Artorias. I am the Regis or King of the North American Vampires." The reporters look unsure about what to make of his statement. A few laugh and make jokes.

The commandos I blasted flank the Regis.

I whipped the personal guard of the vampire big kahuna. Whoops. In my defense, it's not like they wore nametags. I had no idea they were one of the good guys.

One of the commandos catches me staring. I smile apologetically and wave. He smirks and shakes his head. At least there don't appear to be any hard feelings.

"Your government is scheduled to make an announcement following mine. The reason for this press conference is to let you know the world you know is gone. No longer will you live under the illusion humans are the only intelligent species. The supernatural are not myth or legend read about in books. From this day forward know that we're among you. Our kind has lived in relative peace with humans. Recent actions by a handful of persons forced us to step forward. Tonight, we ended their reign of terror over us. We will not be threatened. We can live together, or we can destroy one another. The choice is yours. The American government has assured us cooperation. Together we will work out a plan beneficial to us all. Thank you for your time. No questions, please."

CHAPTER 28

August 31

Rachel

THE FOLLOWING DAYS are tense. True to his word, Manias met with the President of the United States. The Regis has taken up the mantle of the Shadow People's diplomat. The news coined the term Shadow People. Bastien hates it, says it's too trendy sounding.

New laws are written to protect everyone. No shadow person may harm a human without being subject to human law, enforced by Manias. That means even if humans are too weak to force compliance, Manias guarantees he will make it happen. The king keeps many dark creatures at his disposal.

As for the humans, if they break the law, they're off to meet the Tribunal. Facing down a room of Shadow People delegates is no human's idea of a good time.

Most everyone is cooperating to make this work. A program to facilitate a better understanding between our races is coming. The upcoming human generation will be offered classes in school on the history of the supernatural to help separate fact from fiction.

The system is not perfect. A few riots have broken out on

both sides. An underground resistance is brewing. I fear we will see more trouble.

The general public is afraid of me. I'm the wild card in the deck. The Arcane. Doctors want to examine me; Bastien refuses to let them near. I did agree to a debriefing by the government, but on my terms. My shadow world status as Bastien's mate protects me. The powers that be cannot make me comply to their wishes because they fear the repercussions.

The most enlightening developments have been found within the records of The Richland Institute. The Wraiths stole the secrets they were keeping inside. Gates mentioned an insider to me in the limo all those weeks ago, the information the Wraiths obtained points to a traitor among the vampires. Manias is livid, only a small handful of people know about this. Nikolai has sworn to find the spy.

Nikolai brought me my file from Richland, he didn't let Manias or Bastien see it. I earned the Wraith Commander's admiration when I threw him through the roof and then had the gall to smile at him during the press conference.

"We all owe you a debt of gratitude, without you we wouldn't have known about Richland. It's not something we can repay you for, but for what it's worth, thank you. You're a warrior worthy of praise, whatever secrets are in here, they're your secrets," he said.

I hugged him; I couldn't help myself.

"Will Manias be mad if he finds out you kept this file from him?" I ask.

The Wraith smiled roguishly and said, "He'd have to find me first."

I decided to read the file before showing it to Bastien. Inside, I found details of my early life and family. A newspaper clipping from the debacle when I was a child featured an interview from my old Pastor; he called me unnatural and possessed by spirits of foretelling. I think that's how I got on Richland's radar. Surveillance photos, embarrassingly detailed reports from Anna starting from the first night she made contact with me, and the brain activity test she insisted I take are included.

My memories are still scattered, which is no wonder considering how many times they fed me the drugs to reset my brain. I doubt I'll ever recall my life before waking up in Richland clearly. The memories I have are dreamlike, I know things like my birthday, where I was born, and my parents' names but I can't tell you about my first date or the family vacation we took when I was fourteen.

The memory center of my brain is swiss cheese.

After reading the file for himself, Bastien kissed me and promised to make new memories together.

The Bonvillian family is recovering. No one wants to breathe for fear it will upset the balance. Bastien is withdrawn. The discovery that Athan is alive rocked the family. He's alive, but lost to them. It's a bitter pill to swallow. Adele took it hardest. One day, I found her watching Livia while she played chess with Claude. She looked so sad. She caught me staring and hastily left the room. I followed her, never one to let well enough alone.

"Adele, wait. Talk to me?"

She tries to wave me off. "Why? I'm never kind to you. Why would you want to know my troubles?"

Smiling, I shrug. "I'm stubborn. I don't give up."

"Not a bad quality," she chuckled. "When I lost Athan, it devastated me. I let the pain of losing one child get in the way of caring for my Sebastien and Madalaina. Then they were gone too. I've made so many mistakes. How do I ever make it right?"

"You may not be able to. You can't change your past, but don't make more mistakes on top of the old ones. Livia is your second chance. Be her grandmother. Over time, Bastien and Madalaina may come around when they see the effort you are making with their niece."

"I can understand why my son took you as a mate," she praises. "Perhaps one day we will be able to mend what I have broken"

"Sure. Just don't vote for my execution anymore," I say.

Adele has a charming laugh.

Athan still hasn't come home. It's been two months since the siege. Bastien waits for him every day. He sits on the front steps of the Bonvillian house. His loyalty is inspiring, but I can't let him continue. Each night when he finally comes to our bed, he's exhausted emotionally. He gathers me in his arms and holds me while I sleep, but he never sleeps. I despise Athan a little more each day. He has stolen my husband's soul with his absence. I daydream about finding Athan and zapping him until he glows blue. Before I can completely lose it, a letter arrives.

To my family,

I am sorry I continue to stay away. My disappearance causes you pain and my refusal to return causes more. I cannot explain my actions except to say that I am not ready. I've been nearby, watching. I missed much of your lives, and I grieve for the time I lost.

Madalaina has grown into a beautiful woman. Father must be beside himself over the wolves knocking at the door. Father, the wolves stand no chance; guard against mangy cats. I am trying to be the man you would want me to be. Please have patience.

Mother, patience has never been your virtue. You will be mad at me. I can hear you in my head telling me to stop shirking my duties. I love you, Mother. Bastien, stop sitting on the porch. Your beautiful new mate is waiting for you. Don't lose her because you are too busy looking for me. You'll be a great Alpha Prime, I have faith in you. Rachel, thank you. I owe you my freedom. My last message is for Livia. You may choose when she's ready. Livia, I am the man that fathered you, but I cannot be your father. We're genetically linked and will always be a part of each other. I care for you and want you to be safe. I want you to stay with your Uncle Bastien and Aunt Rachel. I suspect over time you will come to know them as your parents. You deserve a happy childhood. I know my brother, he will be a wonderful father. I've watched Rachel with you. She already loves you like a mother. Go and live a remarkable life. One day, maybe we will see each other.

Sincerely,
Athan Bonvillian

The letter provides closure. Adele is surprisingly okay with Athan's choice.

"He's haunted. He does not wish to bring his demons into our home. I would commend any other man for such a choice, why not my own son?" she says.

Claude is visibly saddened, but stands behind his wife's belief that Athan is making the best decision. It is selfish of me, but I am relieved. I do love Livia like my own. Giving her up to Athan would break my heart.

As the Alpha Prime, Bastien must put this behind him. He has too many relying on him. I think knowing Athan is okay, or as okay as he can be, helps lighten his soul. We chose to tell Livia an abbreviated version of Athan's letter. It will be saved for her when she's older. For now, she knows her biological father is Bastien's brother, and he cannot be here to care for her. We asked if she would like to live with us, she cried and threw herself in my arms. She calls me mom. I'm the only mother she has ever known. It was weeks later when she asked Bastien if he thought Athan would mind if she called Bastien dad. He assures her it would be okay with Athan. Bastien tells her he'd be honored if she called him dad. The day I woke up in the white room, I never dreamed it would lead me down a road to family.

CHAPTER 29

Feb 9

Rachel

I AM HAPPY, for once my life is relatively normal. Bastien is occupied with pack affairs and I have been recognized as the alpha female of the pack. A few women tried to push the issue but quickly learned I don't need teeth or claws to force their submission. My Arcana has finally stabilized. Dr. Keller keeps a close watch over me. He's studying all the samples Doctor Morris gave me to ensure they can never be used against us. We all suspect the government had a part in Richland's research. There are too many unanswered questions regarding his funding, but for now, there is peace.

I see Varian Caina when I visit Dr. Keller. He's an odd vampire, sadness surrounds him, but he tries to hide it. He's a friend and is especially fond of Livia. Bastien says he was a recluse before, but since everything went down he's been trying to forge relationships. I hear he spends a lot of time with the Regis and a vampire princess named Tsura. The gossips running the rumor mill swear there will be a wedding alliance between Varian and Tsura, but I don't believe it. I saw how he looked at Winter. I think he still mourns her death.

Madalaina parties too much in an effort to drive off her mother's attempts at affection. I hope they can find a way to work things out. I worry about her, but Bastien assures me she has a constant shadow watching over her, probably Cleary. She misses her friend Winter. Word got passed that the body of a Fae man and woman was found burned beyond recognition. The official report from Fairy claims it was Winter and her cousin Kiril.

My darling Livia is turning six this month. She blossomed so much under the love of her family. She attends a private school and has many friends. Adele was worried she would be an outcast. It never happened. Livia draws people to her like a beacon of light.

Bastien and I are in love. He hasn't spoken the words, but I am confident it's true. I'm not confident about how he will take the news that I'm pregnant. As often as we have sex I can't imagine he will be surprised. I'm stalling. Nerves flutter in my stomach. Livia is playing in her room.

"Rachel, can I talk to you in the bedroom?"

I think Bastien suspects something is up. When we're alone, he looks at me expectantly.

"Mind telling me what is going on? You are wound tighter than a cat in a room full of rocking chairs."

"How can you tell?"

"You spin the bracelet I got you when something is on your mind." He grins.

I look down at my wrist, sure enough I'm twirling the silver fleur-de-lis infinity bracelet round and round by the royal blue cord. The fleur-de-lis charm matches the tattoo on Bastien's arm and the infinity symbol represents our future together, he gave it to me on the one-month anniversary of our mating.

"I'm pregnant," I blurt out.

Bastien turns green. He gently lays a hand on my stomach. "Are you okay? Have you seen a doctor?"

"I'm healthy. We're healthy. Dr. Keller says, other than a slightly quicker development, our baby is fine. Right on target for shifter babies. He doesn't think what Richland did to me will adversely affect the baby."

He touches his forehead to mine, "Thank God. I can't lose you Rachel. I love you too much to ever be without you."

Tears fill my eyes. He loves me. "I love you, too. Are you happy about the baby?"

"I'm overjoyed."

His lips touch mine in the sweetest kiss. Through the mate bond, I feel his love for me. Intense and true, mirroring my own.

"Let's go tell Livia she's going to be a big sister." He grins at me.

"Don't forget your Mom and Dad."

Bastien groans. "Mom is going to be a pain in the ass, you know that, right? You've seen her with Livia. I won't be surprised if she sets up guard in the baby's room."

This moment is perfect. I close my eyes to permanently etch it into my memory. I can't wait to see what the future holds.

WINTER'S KISS
WORLD IN SHADOWS 1.5

CHAPTER 1

October 14

Varian

DREAMS ARE THE ONE PLACE you can't lie to yourself. Humans are notorious for pretending everything in their life is great, but they suffer from the harsh reality of their nightmares each time they close their eyes. The ones that can't even begin to reconcile their fantasies with the real world are driven mad by insomnia. A human life span is too long for any creature to endure such a fate, but a vampire's life span is significantly longer. I vowed to take a realistic view of my life so that at least in dreams I would always find peace. A good plan as long as you don't allow yourself to become connected to others. I learned the hard way that some things will haunt you even if you're brave enough to look them in the face.

I avoided sleep as long as I could after Winter ditched me. She bolted from the Seelie Queen Tanith with her cousin Kiril in tow. I'd thought myself immune to the trappings of intimate relationships, but Winter stirred emotions in me over the course of a few days that no other had managed to do in the centuries before her. I saw a future with children, adorable like their mother and mischievous like me, a dream I'd given up a long time ago. Happiness in my grasp and torn away after a taste.

I sound maudlin, someone please shoot my ass before I begin waxing rhapsodic about her lavender hair.

Tell yourself you're fine and you've moved on, but when you dream you'll uncoverthe truth. I've run the gamut of emotions: anger, depression, and denial. Denial's a popular choice. What's that saying? Oh yes, denial isn't just a river in Egypt.

Firefly deserted me. Who needs her?

Me, I need her.

My dreams torment me with what could've been, perpetually ending with Winter's unexpected retreat. I'd have stayed in dreams forever if it meant she'd still be alive. In October Queen Tanith announced the two bodies burned to charcoal briquettes were Winter and Kiril. The pain in my heart was physically staggering. I blamed Tanith. So she didn't strike the match, but she's the reason they ran to begin with. If they hadn't, they might still be alive. Weeks before I threatened retaliation in the event Winter was harmed, but I couldn't do it. I spent the majority of my life in solitary confinement at the request of my people; they say I'm too dangerous.

Isn't that the point? We're vampires, dangerous is our thing.

I could've forced the issue; no one could *make* me do anything I didn't want to. I did refuse for a time, but the protesters made Manias' life a living hell. We've been friends since boyhood, and his reign, as king hasn't made him forget where he came from. Manias fought for my freedom, and me, so I decided to go with it. The community at large already ostracized me.

Why make an effort to be around people who don't want me?

Winter changed everything. She came crashing into my life like a tidal wave, and washed the slate clean. With her I found a reason to do more than just exist. Without her I lost more than I ever knew I had. When she died I'd wanted to burn the world down in my rage, but instead I faced a deep depression that sucked the life from my body. My will died with Winter.

This melancholy emo shit is irritating.

If I'd stop pouting and go blow up someone, I'd cheer up. Roasted Tanith would be cathartic and I did promise, can't break a promise. The pep talks never worked. I was lost and cared about nothing. I avoided dreams when Winter left, but three days after her death I eagerly anticipated a chance to dream.

This one was strange from the start; the landscape was enveloped in fluffy white snow. Glittering snowflakes floated in a graceful dance with the wind. Winter stood barefoot in the snow, a blue and white dress softly waved around her. Lavender hair unbound, the curls fell longer than I remembered. Despite the frigid temperature I was warm.

"Hello Varian," she spoke softly.

I'd give anything to have her back.

I was afraid to touch her. "I wish this was real," I whispered.

Winter tipped her head to the side and beamed at me.

"I'm here for real, sort of. You're dreaming, but I'm projecting myself into your thoughts."

Kicked in the gut by her remark, my face fell and anger replaced my joy.

She lives?! Why the fuck didn't she contact anyone?!

I crunched across the snow to stand toe to toe with her. "What the hell, Winter! Tanith announces you're death and you wait almost a week to let me know it's a lie?" I roared.

Winter set a hand on my chest and forced me backward. "You're the one who bought her lies! Did you see my body?" She shouted back, poking me in the chest to punctuate each sentence.

Caught off balance by her intensity, I all but fell on my ass. I had to windmill my arms to remain upright. Winter snickered behind her hand at my cartoonish efforts to stay on my feet. Her infectious laughter was sweet; it assuaged my anger. I laughed with her. Winter took it as encouragement to laugh harder, she clutched her stomach and doubled over laughing until she couldn't breathe. I hated to ruin her moment, but we needed to talk. Arms crossed over my chest, I leaned against a tree and regarded her.

"Everyone believes you're dead, Winter. Madalaina Bonvillian mourns deeply for you and Tsura Tymar is more stoic than usual. Don't you think they deserve to know you're alive?"

Winter composed herself and let out an exasperated sigh. "What they deserve is to be protected." She settled her fists on her hips adopting a defensive posture. "Tanith wants me gone because there are rumblings of a revolution. Unsatisfied Fae desire to place me on the throne. She's hunting for me, but so far I've succeeded in eluding her. As long as I stay away, I think Tanith will focus her attention on me and not the ones I love."

What the fuck?!

I threw my hands in the sky gesturing violently I growled, "What about my safety! Don't I rate? You won't go to Madalaina or Tsura because you're terrified Tanith would kill them, but you're fine putting me in danger? Shouldn't you want to keep me safe? Don't you love me?"

Ah shit, did I really just ask her that? Be cool, maybe she didn't notice.

Winter's brow furrowed, she glanced down at the snow. "You're the one person I couldn't stay away from," she murmured. Shaking off the tender moment she slipped into a joke. "Besides, nothing short of a global implosion is liable to kill you." She laughed tensely.

I wouldn't look at her; instead I kicked at the snow with my boot. "I'm not as indestructible as everybody thinks, I'm merely good at bluffing and possess stronger magic than most. Doesn't mean I can't be killed." I cautioned, disturbed and hurt by her disregard.

Winter's grasp on my forearm eases the hurt, my anger diffused. She smoothed her thumb along the skin. Tears sparkled crystalline in her eyes.

"Not what Tanith believes, and that's all that matters right now."

I lowered my arms and tugged her tight against my chest.

We held on to one another for a time. Her head fit perfectly under my chin; she was made for me.

Will we ever have this again?

I asked cautiously, "Will you come back? You can't live your life on the run permanently."

"I don't plan to. I'm looking for pages missing from the Book of Dawns." Her reply was muted by my shirt, her hold on me nearly bruising. I squeezed her closer.

The Book of Dawns had been our trump card when we were trying to escape Tanith after stealing Winter's magic back from the Fae. Tanith was pissed at them. The worst bit is the book claims vampires sprang from the Fae, technically making all vampires Fae.

They need to burn that book, it's embarrassing.

I worked my fingers through her hair, the strands clinging to my hand. "What do you believe is on the missing pages?" I murmured.

Winter inhaled a deep cleansing breath and let it out before answering. "I'm not certain, but I want to know why they're torn out. Hoping for information I can utilize to negotiate with Tanith."

I scoffed "Or I toast the bitch. Problem solved."

Her body quaked in my embrace when she chuckled. "That takes care of Tanith but not her supporters or King Corrigan."

Make me a list.

She heaved a heavy sigh and loosened her hold on me, but I refused to let her escape from my embrace.

"You're leaving already?" I questioned.

She palmed my cheek with her right hand; the warmth

comforted me. I closed my eyes and relaxed into it. "This depletes a lot of my magic. I must be strong in case I run into trouble."

I beseeched her. "Tell me where you are, I can help."

She shook her head. "No, Varian. I won't put you in any more danger than I already have. Please understand."

Helpless to change her mind, I tried another approach. "Give me something, Winter. If I find out you were wounded and I could've assisted, I would never forgive myself."

"You're such a drama queen, you know that Varian?" she rolled her eyes and smirked.

I winked. "You may address me as Her Royal Majesty."

"Fine." Her face turned solemn, "I travel constantly so I can't tell you a location, but I can give you my true name."

Nothing says commitment like a fairy exposing her true name.

I withdrew a step to get a better glimpse into her eyes. "Are you sure you trust me? The Fae guard true names with a fierceness even I admire."

True names are tethers no Fae can disregard. I shout out 'Winter' she can ignore me, but if I whisper her true name in an empty room she'd be compelled to answer.

"I trust you with everything, Varian." Winter tenderly swept my lips with the tips of her fingers. "My true name is Aoife. The only other person who knew it took the secret to his grave."

"Kiril doesn't know?" I asked.

She scoffed, "Absolutely not. Kiril's been a power hungry social climber for as long as I've known him. Helping to save

Livia was extremely out of character for him. Just because he did one good deed doesn't mean he is any different. Now I'm stuck traveling with him, but don't think for a minute I trust him." Her voice echoed farther and farther away, "I should go, the link is fading. I promise to check in soon."

I grimly agreed as I waited for the dream to end.

CHAPTER 2

March 22

Winter

I EXPECTED LIFE to take me on many grand adventures. Adventures sound great, but once I found myself on one all I wanted was to go home. Tanith faked my death and the death of my cousin Kiril. She wanted us cut off from anyone who could provide us with aid. I stayed away from loved ones because I knew Tanith was watching, and I didn't want anyone getting hurt. Kiril didn't know anyone who wouldn't turn him in to Tanith for a pat on the head. Why did I think the missing pages of the book that got me in trouble in the first place could help me?

Hell, could they do anything to worsen my situation?

My crusade to find the missing pages brought me to Ireland. Kiril doesn't like the weather, or food, or people. He complains 24/7, and I ache to sew his lips together. I think he regrets providing me with the book. He lost the social status and perks at Court by helping me. His professed love for his dead sister and her sick child faded once he realized he's not a pampered prince anymore and I was so over listening to him bitch and moan after the first week. He talked about writing a memoir, *the Lament of Kiril*, his rise to glory and subsequent fall.

Please, let Tanith find Kiril when I'm not around and smite him!

Kiril rested on a rock to my right fiddling idly with a blade of grass. "Do we have to be out here in the middle of Podunk Ireland? Can't we go to Dublin?"

I rubbed my forehead and shut my eyes to quell the throbbing in my brain.

"No, because the pages aren't in Dublin. They're in the ruins of one of the five old keeps our ancestors built."

"But whyyyy?"

Whining like a damn child.

Irritation and fatigue got the best of me. I wheeled around on my foot to face him and knelt to eye level. "Kiril, can you please shut your yap for say, five minutes so I can think? Your voice makes me want to smash my face in with a hammer. 'Kay? Thanks."

Not a nice thing to say; but produced the desired effect. Kiril pouted on his rock while I eyed the surface of the third keep on our list of potential hiding places. I didn't want to go in, I just wanted to go home and back to the life I had before.

That's never going to happen, get over it or go crazy.

I looked down at my dirt streaked clothes and muddy boots. Each nail on my hands torn from digging and moving rocks; searching for those damn pages. Getting out of bed in the morning was unpleasant; my muscles ached all over. I could heal and clean up in a wink, but it would leave me vulnerable. My magic is close to being exhausted in an attempt to keep us off Tanith's radar. Last report I heard she'd set Red Caps on our trail, no doubt borrowed from the Unseelie King.

Don't think he'll be willing to grant me asylum if he's loaning troops to Tanith.

The time I spent with Varian five months ago burned me out. It took weeks before I could make a move without fearing we'd be discovered.

The entrance to the ruined keep was still standing despite the fact half of it sunk underground. It was an uncomfortably tight squeeze, but I needed to know if the pages were down there. I decided to go in feet first; didn't want to meet whatever might live here face first. The drop to the sunken great hall wasn't far, but I'd need to jump up to reach the opening when I left or have Kiril help lift me out.

Kiril participate in manual labor? Perish the thought!

I removed the Maglite from my belt loop. It was bright and heavy, and doubled as a weapon. It wasn't likely the pages would be hanging around this close to the exit so I needed to go down into the depths towards the catacombs. Fae kept the best treasure hidden inside the catacombs, a labyrinth of stone hallways meant to keep out human thieves. They'd die of starvation before finding the loot or the way out.

A scurrying behind me made the hairs on my neck rise. I whipped around ready to attack but found no one. Not stupid enough to blame the wind, I inspected the ground and walls.

Tiny tracks in the dirt belonging to a spriggan confirmed precious treasure would be here. Unfortunately so were spriggans; at least one if not more.

Disgusting little bastards.

Spriggans love treasure and can rob you blind in broad daylight and you'd never notice them, they're that good. They're also evil, vindictive, and possess a nasty disposition. Usually small in stature, spriggans can grow enormous. More than one adversary had dismissed them as a threat only to be stomped into the ground. They wouldn't like my presence here.

I shook off my apprehension; I couldn't turn back. Another level down I found a crudely scribbled message in old Fae.

DETH WHAITS BILOW

Lovely. Good to know.

No messages greeted me down the spiral passageway. Fae don't hide their treasures from each other, it's a challenge. Place them in plain sight or a well-known location but guard them. If you're good enough to take it without being caught, it's yours. I didn't have trouble finding the treasure cache, Fae artifacts call to their kinsmen.

It's like they want to get stolen. No wonder Fae don't bat an eyelash at stealing from each other.

A disembodied voice croaked harshly. "Leave now, Seelie bitch or I'll use your pretty skin to line my coat."

I rolled my eyes. Hardly original. "Technically, I'm dual Court. To kill me is to murder a fellow Unseelie."

"You? Unseelie? Ha! You've too many sweet Seelie

manners in you to be regarded as one of us. Besides, I'd kill you all the same. I care not if you were my own mother."

Oh, he's delightful.

I stood unyielding, ready to defend myself. "All I want are the pages from the Book of Dawns. I won't touch anything else."

"Nothing! You'll take nothing! All is mine, MINE!" His shout ricocheted off the walls and jolted me.

"Stop hiding in the shadows, spriggan! Or are you a coward?" I taunted, smiling snidely.

"Muck is not a coward, Seelie bitch!" Scuffling in the dark gave away his position.

Muck? Seriously?

Before he moved to another hiding hole, I blasted shards of ice at him. His yelp assured me I hit my mark. The glow of my flashlight illuminated him, pinned to the stone by the ice. Black pungent blood leached from the wounds. Muck was two feet tall with brown fur covering his body. The fuzz on his head was longer and wildly matted with leaves and slime. Spindly arms and legs too long for his fat body made him look like a spider. The fingers owned an extra knuckle and ended in sharp spines with no nails. His extended forehead hung over his glowing green eyes and flattened nose.

I remembered from my studies as a child that he would have tiny pointed teeth hidden behind thin lips.

"Hello, Muck. I'll be taking my pages now."

Muck struggled to lash out at me, but the ice held fast.

I shouldered open the treasure vault door and gasped. Muck owned an impressive collection, mostly coins and metal bits, but it filled the room floor to ceiling. I didn't have time to sift through it for the pages. Transporting nearby objects to another location is a simple task and requires very little magic. A wave of my hand and anything metallic disappeared from the room; I sent it to the bottom of the lake outside.

Sorry, Muck.

The paper and garb left wasn't difficult to sort. The pages were buried under an ancient coronation gown. The garment was beautiful once, but age and improper care left it in dusty tatters. Thankfully, it had preserved the pages from degrading beyond the point where I could read the text. I knew the pages wouldn't survive once I took them from the ruins. Once they were unshielded by magic they'd disintegrate. Having not been preserved the way the Book of Dawns was, these pages were subjected to the test of time.

Once I crossed the threshold they'd cease to exist. I checked, Muck was still preoccupied with trying to escape. I sagged back against the wall to read.

It came to pass in the time before time, a race of creatures was born of darkness and wrath. Soulless and unfeeling, they fed off the life force of others to sustain their longevity. The life force of a magical species was preferred. When they had exhausted all sentient life on their home world they turned to the planet itself, siphoning off the energy until nothing but a shell remained. It was then that they left their decaying planet in search of other feeding grounds. Eventually, they came upon the birthplace of the Fae, where we lived long before Earth was born. The King and Queen sacrificed themselves to send our whole race into an alternate dimension on Earth. We have existed free of threat ever since, but there will come a time when we can no longer hide. They are master hunters. Empty, hollow beings that leave oblivion in their wake. They are The Unfilled and one day we will face them with nowhere left to run.

"There used to be only one Court? Why the division into Seelie and Unseelie? Who would benefit from these pages being torn out?" I asked myself.

There were references to ancient artifacts that would help discern the signs of The Unfilled's impending arrival. I was familiar with two of the items, but one I'd never heard of. The Star Sphere and Dark Scepter could be found in the castle vaults, one at each Court. Queen Aine's amulet would require more investigation. That's it, answers that do nothing to help me free myself from Tanith's wrath and the promise of a shit storm to come.

Muck's grunts of exertion mixed with the cracking of ice told me I'd used up my time. I dropped the pages and ran for the opening to the catacombs. I seized the stairs but my pace slowed as my side ached and lungs burned from running. I stopped to rest before I passed out. Breathing eased the pain, but gave Muck a chance to catch me. I heard Varian's authoritative voice in my head.

Get your ass in gear, firefly!

I placed my palm to the cold mossy stone wall and ascended the spiral stairs to the great hall. Muck grabbed my ankle and pulled my feet out from under me. The stone bit into my stomach, hips, and chest. He hauled me backward, the cheese grater surface of the steps scraping my chin and right cheek. Furiously screaming and kicking at Muck, I fought for freedom. One of my thrashing feet connected squarely with Muck's face. The second his grip loosened, I drove up and ran into the great hall.

Muck landed on my back, but I didn't go down. One arm coiled around my neck choking me, while the opposite one stabbed at my lower back. Stick like fingers sharp as knives speared through my frame on the lower left side. The burning pain knocked the breath out of me. I couldn't shake him off for fear of his fingers ripping out my side. I waited for him to remove his hand. I flipped Muck overhead and slammed him onto the floor in front of me. Blood surged from the injury in my side.

I don't think I can fix this.

I don't do failure well. I avoid board games and sports because I hate to lose. Muck cut me low, and I didn't think I could escape death at his hands, but I wouldn't let my corpse be a feast for him. Muck crouched on the ancient rushes scattered across the floor, he ridiculed in song.

"Little Seelie, fair and fine, once you fall, your flesh is mine."

I'd failed Madalaina and Tsura, but saddest of all I failed Varian by dying. Tears would wait, first I wanted to deal with the anger. I'd never been so angry.

It's not right. All I've done is help others.

Muck's tittering flung me over the edge. I screamed, and it was dark and guttural. Muck quit laughing. The murky shadows in the chamber moved, slithering like snakes towards us. Light was smothered, but I could see in the black. Guided by my will they swarmed over Muck, his screeches quieted to gurgles, and it delighted me. The darkness retreated, and small beams of sun peeked in between cracks. This new magic was unfamiliar to me, I'd never heard of a Fae of my lineage being able to call shadows.

Muck lay broken among the rushes. He was fatally injured and I knew he'd die any second. He convulsed and more of the unclean mire spewed out.

"Not a pretty Seelie," he wheezed. "Unseelie Royal, calls the Sluagh." More whimpering and crying, none of it moved my heart towards compassion.

I discovered a clean spot on the ground to curl up and stay warm. I called out to Varian.

Please hear me, Varian.

CHAPTER 3

Varian

WAITING FOR WORD from Winter was maddening. Patience is a virtue I want nothing to do with. I'm climbing the walls and it's getting on Keller's nerves. He didn't think I was all that sane on good days, and I'm living up to my reputation as a nutcase with all the pacing and mumbling. I'd tried to wear myself out in the gym downstairs and attempted to distract myself with reading, but no dice. I gave up and headed to my study to call Manias and bother him, when it happened.

Winter's voice was weak, but I felt her call. I didn't waste time; I took the stairs two at a time up to my private suites. No one is allowed to bother me there, not even the Regis himself. I checked all the shutters and doors making sure they were locked tightly before moving to the large open space in my bedroom.

Nerves in my stomach made me want to vomit. I was seconds away from seeing her again in person.

"I call you Aoife." My voice rang out over the room.

I wasn't sure how this true name calling crap worked, I hoped I did it right. Less than a minute passed before Winter materialized in the room, but it seemed like years. Soaked in blood with various cuts and contusions on her body, she appeared on her feet but collapsed when the transfer finished. I fell to my knees and caught her. Cradling her in my arms, her shallow breathing worried me.

I stroked the hair off her face. "Fuck me! Winter, who did this to you?" I cried hoarsely.

"Spriggan." She winced. "Dead now."

I laid a kiss on her forehead. "Atta girl."

She raised her hand to touch my cheek; a tear glistened on her finger. I didn't know I was crying.

Smiling weakly she asked, "Do you remember when you asked if I loved you?"

"Heard that did you?" I chuckled.

The ghost of a smile touched her lips. "Yeah. Did you mean it?"

My breath shuddered, my chest tight. "I meant it, you're the one for me."

"I love you too." She whispered, and I felt her slipping away.

Damn it, no! Why am I always losing this woman?

Binding Winter to me was the only way to bring her back. Vampire binding spells remove half of the soul from each partner, exchanging the souls to bind them together. Bound couples share a blended soul keeping them tethered together. After I bound Winter to me, she'd be a part of me in a literal sense. Our feelings, thoughts, even dreams, a shared experience, not a bargain to be entered into lightly. If it had been anyone else, I'd let her die.

The process itself isn't spectacular; souls aren't tangible

things you can see. I knew of a few times a couple had allowed witnesses at a binding, but they hadn't found it noteworthy. The binding of souls was felt and not seen. There are no special words or ritual to perform. I needed to look inside myself and find the part of me that called to her—my soul. Once found I would tear it in half, because love isn't without sacrifice. I hadn't expected the breaking of my soul to be emotional, but I was devastated.

So much for being the hardened, uncaring monster people think I am.

The soul fragment would search for the soul of my devotion and bond to it. If Winter felt the same her soul would offer up its own fragment, at least that's the idea. It felt like ages waiting for her soul to make a decision. I was raw and reeling inside. Winter's soul fragment jumped into me, smoothed the ragged edges of what remained of mine and fused into one. Instantly I felt contentment, quiet peacefulness stilled the raging waters crashing restlessly inside me. Maybe I'd had this feeling on my own once, but I couldn't remember. Winter gasped and sat straight up coming out of my arms too fast for me to move and slammed her head into my nose.

"Fuck me! Don't mangle the face, firefly!" I shouted.

Winter sat on the floor, hands clasped to her chest and eyes closed tight.

She grimaced, "A bottle tossed into a stormy sea, a tempest inside me."

I smiled apologetically. "Yeah, sorry, my half of your soul. Yours is great though."

Her eyes snapped open and pinned me on the spot. In one fluid motion, she rose to her full height. I scurried backward in an awkward crab walk; she looked menacing. My back hit the bedroom wall, nowhere else to go. She stopped in front of me and crouched down. Her smile was feral.

"Why do I have half of your soul inside me, Varian?" Her voice was sticky sweet, but the wildness in her eyes was too angry to mistake.

Shit. Calm collected Winter is now only half calm...the other half is crazy ass me.

"I didn't know another way to save you," I explained. "I bound us to give you strength and life, you'll be more powerful now. We're a united force."

Winter shot to her feet and kicked me in the ribs. It hurt, but she didn't use enough force to break anything.

Positive sign!

Winter thrust her hand up into her hair and pulled in frustration. "You bound us!! Damn you to hell, Varian. What about what I want? Did you stop to think about me?!" She yelled down at me, hands on her hips now.

I stopped trying to be playful, I shook my head and said "Truthfully, no. I was done losing you to death, woman. I love you, and you said you love me so what the hell? It wouldn't have worked if you didn't have the same feelings for me. Is being bound to me so bad?"

Her stance relaxed, she sighed rubbing at her forehead and walked over to sit on my bed. I stayed on the floor, not wanting to get kicked again.

"Soul bound to you isn't so bad, no. I'm always in danger,

and I don't want to take you down with me. I can't handle knowing I might get killed. This is frustrating as hell."

She's cute when she's frustrated.

Watch out, asshole. I can hear you now.

Mind sharing wasn't something that happened all the time, but if you didn't make an effort to keep the other out they'd hear it all.

"If I come over and sit with you, are you gonna hit me again?" I teased.

"You'll just have to take the risk," She replied flatly.

I waggled my eyebrow at her. "Oooh, I do like to live dangerously." I crossed the room to stand by the bed.

"Shackled yourself to me," Winter huffed. "Ought to be plenty to keep you on your toes."

I pulled Winter to her feet and hugged her. "I've lost you too many times, no more."

"Well then, guess that's settled." She chuckled. "If you wanted to cuddle you could've just asked."

My turn to tease. "Forget cuddling, this is an attempt to save my bed. You're dripping blood all over."

"Not my fault, you can't blame the bleeder. If you'd like to take the issue up with Muck, he's a heap of disgusting mess back in a ruined Irish castle. Be my guest." She gestured to the door with her hand.

One less enemy I have to kill.

"You should probably tell me what happened. Did you find what you were looking for?" I questioned.

Winter gently banged her head repeatedly on my chest

and groaned. "Oh man did I ever. I opened a can of worms, turned out to be monster titan boas."

She did say she would come with lots of excitement.

Winter relayed the events inside the ruins. The Unfilled were new to me, but they sounded problematic. The artifacts in the Seelie and Unseelie vaults would have to be stolen. Winter worried we wouldn't be able to break into the vaults without getting caught. I told her to trust me. I devised a two-part plan; part one keep the monarchs busy with chaos and political shit.

There are plenty of mercenaries and Fae with low morals and empty pockets willing to play interference for the money I'm willing to shell out. While the royal pricks are busy, send in two master thieves simultaneously. It'd take time, the plans wouldn't shape up overnight, and we'd need patience.

Winter told me about Muck's attack. Most of her injuries already healed, and the rest would be fine before the day was out. My magic healed her while hers shielded our location from Tanith. I wished Muck had lived, I wanted to kill him myself for what he did to Winter.

"He claimed I called the Sluagh on him." She laughed.

"Only the Unseelie monarch can call the Sluagh, they won't answer to anyone else." I said, incredulously.

Winter waved a dismissive hand. "The Sluagh aren't shadows, they're an army of undead warriors. I've only seen drawings of them as a child since King Corrigan hasn't had any use for them in centuries. It wasn't the Sluagh. Whatever they were, it's gotta be new skill for me,"

What Unseelie magic did she tap into?

"Describe it to me." I encouraged her.

"Oily shadows, blotted out all light, but I could see. Muck was attacked and killed. Then they left." She shrugged.

"Holy shit! You commanded the Sluagh army, Winter! Not the whole thing but the lesser foot soldiers. If they came because you called, then they aren't coming when King Corrigan calls." I watched the myriad of emotions pass over Winter's face, shock, then fear, and finally she turned a little green around the gills.

She groaned and closed her eyes, "No wonder he's loaning Red Caps to Tanith."

"He's pissed at you for taking his greatest army." I started laughing.

Winter smiled indulgently at my laughing fit. "Uncle Corrigan never liked me anyway." A thoughtful tilt of her head, she asked, "Do you think I could call them again, anytime I wanted?"

My laughter died. "Don't try now!" I shouted.

Winter batted her eyelashes at me. "Why Varian, are you afraid of the Sluagh?" she teased.

"Hell yes, I'm afraid of the Sluagh! An undead spirit army of the worst sinners and demons trapped in purgatory—who wouldn't be afraid? I have some self-preservation, you know."

Winter sobered up. "Speaking of preserving yourself, what are we going to do about Blood Moons? I can't promise I'll be available for every one."

Blood Moons are the one time a vampire must feed. A bound couple can only feed from each other or from a person trusted by the couple. She'd feel when I fed, and if the donor made her jealous or angry her emotions would cloud mine. Vampire bonds are a whole new level of possessive.

"Can you think of anyone you'd be okay with me feeding on?"

Winter growled softly.

"I know, I don't like it either, but if you don't make the right choice I'll feel your distaste and be unable to feed. That's dangerous for everyone."

"Bloodlust." She whispered on a shudder.

Very few vampires experienced bloodlust anymore. Back before we were organized under a Regis, vampires relied on themselves to hunt without getting caught. The Blood Moon is when we are the hungriest, and ignoring it sets a vampire off on a rampage of blood and sex. Once there was a rogue vampire in the grip of bloodlust, back in the days when America was young, destroyed an entire village. Wraiths were sent in to take him down, and the Regis had to clean up his mess in a little town called Roanoke.

"I don't know that I can, Varian. The idea of anyone in your arms makes me want to hit something."

"Just not me." I mumbled.

Winter leaned back and punched me playfully in the shoulder. "Not funny! I'm serious. I guess you'll have to pull me out of wherever by calling my true name."

Rubbing at the spot I said, "Works for me. I prefer not to feed from anyone but you, anyway."

Winter sprang out of my arms. "Shit! Kiril, I left him outside the ruins when I went looking for the pages. He's probably dead by now, the big priss."

I watched her curiously. "You don't sound particularly upset at the prospect of his death."

Lips curled in disgust, she shrugged. "If someone doesn't kill him soon, I might."

Her blasé attitude concerned me.

Winter's always been caring, damned near a bleeding heart. Was this change my fault?

She scrubbed her face with both hands and moaned. "I can't do it, I have to know he's okay."

Relieved, I flirted with her. "I had such plans for you this evening. They involved ravishment and debauchery."

Horrified shock, she pretended to gag. "I'm covered in blood and dirt!"

I smiled wide to show off my elongated canines. "Vampire, remember? Blood isn't a turn off, and dirt means we get to shower together."

Heat flashed in her eyes, and I saw my first glimpse of the passion hiding inside Winter. I could have persuaded her to stay with little effort on my part, but if something did happen to Kiril it'd hurt Winter.

I groaned, knowing I was missing heaven on Earth. "Come on, firefly. Let's go round up Kiril."

CHAPTER 4

Winter

SOUL BOUND, humans would call it marriage. I'm married to the most notorious vampire alive, and to think I was worried my life would be dull, wandering the countryside looking for pages. I felt conflicted about our union. The soul bond saved my life, and for that I was grateful.

The problem lies in the huge step in an already complicated relationship.

Varian and I scarcely know each other, we haven't talked outside of a crisis.

Being soul bound, we're united in a way you can't escape. I don't want the bond dissolved, but not having a say irked me. The circumstances were extreme, I understand. I'd get over it soon, and would have already except; Varian's share of my soul made me less forgiving. I liked to believe I was a serene person before, now I'm jumpy as hell and want to stab someone.

No patience for me, shouldn't screw up my life too much. Yeah, right.

Varian teleported us back to Ireland to look for Kiril.

Teleport. It sounds ridiculously sci-fi but it's the best word for what he does, traveling without physically crossing the distance.

We checked the ruins and our campsite Kiril was AWOL.

Why didn't you stay put, Kiril?

I carefully looked for tracks, "Damn you, Kiril. Where the hell are you?" I muttered.

Varian picked through my tent, his mouth curved in aversion. "You've been living here, firefly? It's um, rather rustic."

I narrowed my eyes and pointed a finger at him. "Stow it, fang boy. Not all of us can live in the lap of luxury." I snapped.

"Whoa! Easy, slugger." Varian backed up, hands held high in surrender.

This sucks. How's Varian so perky?

My hand exploded out and seized Varian's waistband. I hauled him over and studied him thoroughly. "We've got the same soul, why am I eager to break a table and you're cool as a cucumber?"

Varian grinned impishly. "I'm used to the 'roid rage feeling, you aren't. Likewise, the chill demeanor is normal for you and I'm fighting the urge to skip like a school girl."

My lips twitched, but I smothered it behind a cough. "If you start skipping, I'm not accountable for my actions." I warned him and released his pants.

"My, those grapes are mighty sour," he teased. He couldn't resist the opening to rib me over our Freaky Friday character switch.

Varian accompanied me to the woods as I abandoned camp to search the forest for Kiril.

I ignored him it would be safer that way.

To locate Kiril I summoned Will-O-The-Wisps to lead me. Diminutive colored lights hovered on the air and led us far into the woods. The proximity of the forest to a Fae ruin worried me. The ruins held a power that drew Fae so the woods likely provided shelter to nymphs, pixies, and gnomes. Fortunately for us, nicer breeds of Fae to run into, and I mean nicer as they won't kill you just for entering their space. If we met an erlking it'd be a painful encounter. Erlkings or alder kings are a ruthless bunch, dragging travelers to their demise.

The Will-O-The-Wisps stayed outside a darker range of forest and wouldn't go beyond.

I nodded my agreement. "I understand, I'm on my own. Thank you for lighting the way." The Will-O-The-Wisps preformed a merry dance before flitting off.

Jaw held tight, Varian investigated the trees. "Whatever dwells here isn't pleasant," he said softly.

I bit my lower lip and remembered all the Fae capable of claiming the forest. I didn't want to be surprised. "I sense it too. We'll be cautious and as nonthreatening as possible."

Varian snickered and plucked at my shirt. "Winter, your clothes are covered in gore and Muck, literally. You can't be nonthreatening in your current state."

I counted to ten in my head and took a deep breath.

"Okay, fine. The new plan is find Kiril, kick ass, and shower. Better?" I stomped off with Varian behind me, I might've detected laughter but attempted to overlook it.

Decapitating your husband on day one is frowned on, even by Fae standards.

Wolves prowled the outskirts of the shadowy forest but avoided the heart. The sense that Varian was a more dangerous predator than they were, kept them at bay.

We found Kiril sagged against a downed tree. He lay limp but beamed affectionately at his captor, a nude woman with flaxen hair. Well, she resembled a naked woman from the front. I caught glimpse of her back, a huldra. Huldra don't have a back, instead the space looked like a hollowed out tree. You could put your hand in and feel the empty space where a heart and lungs should be. Anatomy isn't the same for creatures of magic. Resting over the curve of their buttocks is a cow tail. The pretty hair, sweet face, and perfect breasts lured men into the trap. A huldra craves sexual satisfaction, if their prey delivered; death was delayed. Failure put them in the grave.

No pressure, Kiril.

Life with a huldra isn't a reward; you become no better than a pet or worse, a slave. Kiril isn't dumb and should've known to get a good look at his girlfriend from all angles. Obviously the tail and tree back make it harder to lure your prey, but that's where the uber lovely visage and hauntingly beautiful voice come in handy.

I approached with caution, speaking to Kiril like a child. "Kiril, let the pretty huldra go."

His body remained motionless, but eyes clouded with confusion, glanced at me. "What? Signe isn't a huldra. Are you my sweet?"

"Of course not darling." She cooed and stroked his face.

She's doesn't believe we're a threat, how insulting.

I advanced on her, clenched fists and nostrils flaring. "Bitch, I'll strangle you with your cow tail, back off!" I growled.

Signe snarled over her shoulder. Her back creaked and she flicked her tail wildly.

I heard Varian in my mind. *"Egads, that wasn't attractive! Why couldn't Kiril have seen that?"*

It's Kiril, enough said.

Lifting my right hand in front of me I manifested fire in my upraised palm.

"How'd you like a fireball in that broke tree you call a backside? Does it burn like kindling? Let's find out!"

Signe hissed at the fire and spat at me. "He's mine!" She petted Kiril's hair, smiling at him. "I find him most satisfying."

"Gross." Varian thought.

I'm gonna puke.

A twinkle of mischief shined in Varian's gaze. "You could call the Sluagh and make them handle it." Varian interjected.

Peals of laughter tumbled out of Signe's throat. It caressed my ear like a lover's promise. Of course it was pleasant since the huldra utilize their voice to seduce much like Sirens.

"Only King Corrigan can call the Sluagh," Signe smirked.

"Damn, I was counting on her believing the bluff." Varian thought to me. *"Really don't want to be on the same hemisphere when you hang out with your Sluagh buddies, firefly."*

Wuss

"Yes ma'am. Sluagh bring out the wuss in anyone with a working brain cell."

The second time I summoned the Sluagh was easier than the first. The quickening of my heart pulsed in time with the encroaching shadows. Signe scanned the forest nervously. Varian braced for battle at my side. Hoof beats pounded the ground, war cries echoed, and unearthly torchlights grew brighter.

Signe covered up her ears. "Stop! Stop! You can have him, just make it stop!" she screamed.

Easier said than done.

The Sluagh existed on bloody warfare and soul stealing. Comprised of unrepentant sinners and demons, they reveled in the horrors of war. These were not the lesser foot soldiers I'd met in the ruins with Muck, I recognized them as the Sluagh Army from my childhood nightmares.

Who am I trying to kid? The Sluagh still make appearances in my nightmares.

Riding pale horses, soldiers of the Sluagh took souls from the living. I didn't know how the shadow Sluagh I called this afternoon operated, but the army headed my way would expect me to give them instructions and offer at least one soul as tribute.

Signe ran away, I stood watching the advancing army shoulder to shoulder with Varian.

What've I done?

Varian caught my hand in his. "You've got to talk to Balor. I don't fancy the idea of losing my soul, and I wager Kiril would agree if he was lucid."

The demon king, Balor, had secured his position as the general of the Sluagh after the hero Lugh blinded him at the

Battle of Magh Tuireann. I freed my hand from Varian's and proceeded to meet the Sluagh. I steeled myself for my first encounter with Balor. I had one opportunity to prove myself worthy of his loyalty.

I forced the tremor from my voice and spoke, "Greetings, Balor."

Balor wore dull black armor and sat high upon his warhorse. He raised the visor of his headpiece and inclined his head to me; his voice was surprisingly sophisticated. "Corrigan is no longer king? You've overthrown his rule?" he asked.

I swallowed the lump of nerves in my throat and shook my head. "Not quite. Corrigan lives and he's still the king."

The gauze over Balor's eyes was covered in blood and dirt. The rumor is he's kept the same bandage since the injury was delivered. It amazed me a blind man could lead an undead army so efficiently.

Balor isn't just any blind man.

Balor's lips contorted into what I think was a smile for him, exposing yellowed shark teeth. "I'm pleased to learn I didn't miss witnessing his head cleaved from his neck, but he can't be king. You called the Sluagh, and we came, the transfer of power must have shifted. Don't you bear the mark, Isa rune?" He queried.

I didn't comprehend what he spoke of. "Last time I checked, I was free of runes."

"Look again." Balor suggested. "Whatever door you opened to unlock your potential also allowed you the power to summon the Sluagh. Once you did that you usurped Corrigan from his throne, but you have to complete the transfer of power. To finish the transfer of sovereignty, Corrigan must die or yield to your right. The rune of Isa appears on the rightful Unseelie ruler. Somewhere on your body you should find it. When it appeared on you it faded on Corrigan. Believe me, he knows what you've done."

Peachy freaking keen! Like I don't have enough to do. Corrigan's painting a bright red target on my back as we speak.

I forgot why I should fear Balor, my agitation outweighing my common sense. I punted a rock nearby and sent it sailing through the torso of a Sluagh soldier. The warrior glowered at me and his brothers in arms guffawed forcibly. I cringed, but Balor dismissed the matter with a shrug.

Bad form hurling rocks through your troops.

I propped my right hand on my hip, tipping my head up at Balor. "What if Corrigan kills me first, what happens then?" I asked.

"Then the power returns to him. Try not to die."

Varian cleared his throat noisily reminding me about my shortage of souls to trade.

I endeavored to maintain the friendly conversational tone Balor and I had fostered. "I don't have a soul to offer you. I'm still discovering my capabilities, this morning I could barely call the lesser Sluagh." The damn trembling in my voice returned exposing my anxiety. "I confess I didn't expect it would work when I summoned you."

Balor leaned back in his saddle. "I'll offer a bargain, kill Corrigan and deliver his soul to me. Once this is done, your debt to the Sluagh will be repaid."

I gulped, my eyes widened is shock. "I...I...I accept."

Not that I have much choice.

The signal for the Sluagh to withdraw sounded and the troops begrudgingly pulled out. Balor swung his horse to accompany them, over his shoulder he shouted, "It would be wise to refrain from requesting the Sluagh in the future unless you possess proper tribute, Queen Winter."

The shadows subsided leaving the three of us in the woods alone, Signe nowhere in sight. With the huldra gone, Kiril was slowly coming out of the spell he was placed under. He blinked rapidly and shook his head to clear the fog.

"My head, why is my brain trying to bust out?" he wailed, seizing both temples between his palms.

"Because you're an idiot!" I shouted and kicked the sole of his foot.

"Ow!" Kiril dragged his legs to his chest. He settled back into the pout I recognized so well. "If she starts nagging, kill me Varian."

Varian jammed his hands in his pockets and rocked back on his heels laughing. "No can do, buddy. Gotta keep the little missus happy."

Kiril's eyes were round as saucers, darting back and forth between Varian and me.

I rolled my eyes and waved my hand around. "Yeah, yeah, we're soul bonded, it's a beautiful thing. Now can we please leave the creepy forest of death?" I didn't wait for a reply, I was going whether they followed or not.

Behind me I overheard Varian say to Kiril, "Isn't she awesome?"

CHAPTER 5

Winter

BACK AT THE CAMPSITE, Kiril disappeared into his tent to lick the wounds of his pride. Varian announced he needed to attend to some errands, but he'd return in an hour. I used the opportunity to wash in the lake while I had some privacy. Nothing Fae lived in the lake, or maybe they weren't home at the moment. I thanked my lucky stars either way. I soaked the blood and debris from my skin. Removing the gunk in my hair with what little shampoo I had left. My teeth chattered from the chilled water. Satisfied I was clean, I toweled off and dressed in a pastel pink cotton t-shirt and pajama pants with little lambs on them. My clean clothes are a testament to my vanity. I've been using magic to keep them from getting grungy.

I don't want to run around looking like a hobo, so sue me.

Candlelight inside my tent illuminated the darkness; Varian cast a shadow moving around inside. During my trek back to camp, I thought about my troubles. I had no resolution to any of them, and if I had any chance of leading a happy life with Varian I needed one.

Why can't I fast forward past all the trials that lie ahead?

I'd study The Unfilled, and then what? Tanith and

Corrigan would never let me go. I was too great a threat, my death sentence already signed and sealed. Corrigan would have to be dealt with, or the Sluagh would come banging on my door. The thought of ruling the Unseelie shook me. I wasn't ready to put too much consideration into what it meant for my future. If I was Unseelie Queen, Tanith might elect to attempt peace, but I'd constantly be looking over my shoulder.

What about my children? I can't allow a menace like Tanith to remain once I had kids to defend.

If I indicated plans to seize both Courts, it'd be all out war. There would be countless losses, some of them good Fae who merited better fates. I'm not willing to throw my hat into the arena now. One throne at a time.

I entered the tent and pasted on a smile for Varian.

He crossed his arms and shook his head at me. "Why are you even trying to hide your worries from me, Winter?"

"Habit, I guess." I half smiled at him.

He checked me out from head to toe, and I flushed under his intense scrutiny. My damp hair hung loose, my shirt clung to my curves, resting just above my bellybutton leaving a band of skin on my stomach exposed. His passionate gaze sharpened on my breasts, I could feel my nipples tighten, not on account of the cool air either.

Varian crooked a finger at me. "Come here, Winter. I need to check for lingering injuries."

I just bet you do.

Unsteady legs bore me towards Varian of their own volition. Sex isn't unfamiliar, but Varian and I share the soul bond now. This is uncharted territory for both of us. Varian and I stood facing each other, a scant few inches dividing us. Smoothing my hair off my shoulder, he tenderly cupped my left cheek.

"You're the most beautiful woman I've ever known." He whispered.

I opened my mouth to object, but he cut me off.

"Don't argue or challenge my sincerity because there's never been another woman I would willingly sacrifice everything for. I love you with my heart and soul."

I shut my eyes and opened myself fully to Varian's soul. He *did* think I was the most beautiful woman he'd ever known. He also believed I was made to be his and no others. He didn't just love me because he found me beautiful; he loved everything that *was* me. The soul bond granted him access to intimate parts of my being, and he cherished them all. I realized I loved him the same way; our love was beautiful and rare. The intensity with which we loved broke my resolve.

A sob burst through my lips. Varian gathered me to his chest where I cried, overwhelmed by everything. Varian provided a safe harbor to let my guard down. He rubbed circles on my back until my weeping subsided. Embarrassed, I twisted out of his arms to dry my eyes. I hunted up a tissue to blow my nose.

Awesome, Winter. Blowing your nose after crying all over him is super sexy.

I mentally reprimanded myself, a noise of disapproval clued me in he'd eavesdropped on my thoughts. The tissue was discarded in the trash, and I prepared for a heavy conversation.

Varian had other ideas.

He clasped me by the middle rotating me to face him, and kissed me hard. My fingertips danced into his soft blond locks, grown nearly to his mid-back since the last time we kissed, the day we saved Livia Bonvillian's life together.

I coaxed his lips apart and teased his tongue with mine; I loved how he tasted. I moaned and he growled. The kiss deepened, Varian feasted at my mouth. He lifted me and I wrapped my legs around his waist. I wanted the obstacles between us gone; no shirts or pants in the way.

Too many clothes!

Shh. Slow down, firefly. We only have one first time.

Varian abandoned my lips in favor of my neck, he licked, and sucked, and nibbled down to the collar of my shirt. My nose was buried in his silky hair, he smelled like citrus and the white tea he favored.

"What the hell?" Varian said and abruptly dumped me to my feet. He tore my shirt a few inches to probe my right collarbone. "You've got the motherfucking mark of Isa."

I couldn't see the mark; I lurched to my duffel bag and pulled out a compact mirror. He was right. The rune of Isa, a thick black circle with a vertical blue line in the center, adorned my skin. The image wasn't dark, but somehow I knew it would be in stark contrast against my skin once I cemented my claim to the Unseelie throne.

Varian tipped my chin up to look at him. "The Sluagh, the rune of Isa, Winter you're the heir to the Unseelie throne. Corrigan has to accept you as Queen if he wants to live."

I frowned at Varian, carried his hand from my chin to hold for comfort. "It doesn't matter if he accepts me or not, I'm sworn to Balor and the Slaugh to kill Corrigan and deliver his soul. It was the deal for leaving us in the forest without a soul as tribute."

Varian dropped his head, and hair slipped over his eyes. We sat in silence. He was deliberately shielding his thoughts from me.

He swiped the hair out of his eyes with his free hand and sighed.

"Then we'll kill him."

"It won't be easy, Varian."

Varian beamed ear to ear, "Is anything with us ever easy?"

"No, I suppose it's not."

"I should leave, Winter. The longer I stay, the more likely someone will notice my absence. I can't risk your safety to satisfy my desire for you. But before I go, I need you to promise you'll be safe." He wasn't kidding any longer; he wanted my vow not to die again.

I kissed his cheek and cuddled him close. "I'll be as safe as I can, love."

Varian squeezed me until I couldn't breathe before setting me free. He motioned to outside the tent, "Then consider this a gift. I anonymously contacted the Haltija's, to discreetly protect you. A Raudan Väki has sworn fealty to you."

Varian raised the cover for me to exit the tent, outside was a giant Fae warrior. Tall and built like a brick house, his red hair was braided at the temples, iron gauntlets, and a heavy iron torque glinted under the moon.

A Fae immune to iron is worth his weight in gold.

Haltija's are Unseelie Fae that live to guard or defend. They're loyal until death to no one but their sovereign. Haltija's have a specialty, such as wood, water, or fire. Raudan Väki means Haltija of Iron. Their mission in life consumes every bit of self; Raudan Väki was his station and his name. He could open old wounds delivered by iron, heal an injury created by iron and is immune to iron. Fae are adverse to iron, having him around could prove useful.

I smiled widely at his generosity. "I don't know what to say, thank you."

I extended a hand to the Raudan Väki in greetings but he knelt and bowed his head. "I'm honored to protect you with my life, my queen."

"Let's hope it doesn't come to that, Raudan Väki. Please, call me Winter." I placed my hand on his shoulder encouraging him to rise.

He nodded solemnly and said, "You can call me Raudan."

Varian wasn't used to such praise, he shrugged it off as no big deal. "Well, I can breathe a little easier knowing someone is watching your back."

I'm gonna miss him. Don't cry, don't cry.

I pounced on top of him, toppling him to the ground with me. Raudan smirked and turned his back to grant us privacy.

"I wish you didn't have to leave." I whined. Kiril would've been proud but he was still too busy pretending we didn't exist, sulking inside his tent.

Varian rolled me to my back and kissed my forehead. "It's only two weeks to the Blood Moon, we'll be together again before we know it."

I grumbled, "Two weeks is too long."

Varian placated me with ways to bide our time apart. "I'll figure out a game plan for stealing the artifacts, and put out feelers for allies. You learn what you can about Queen Aine's amulet."

Despite my struggles, the tears came. "This isn't how I imagined the first night with my husband."

Varian cleared the dampness with his thumbs; his voice wavered. "We're going to be together for a long time Winter. This time separated won't be but a blink of an eye to us."

I prayed to any god who was listening he was right.

CHAPTER 6

April 1

King Corrigan

I PACED THE COLD STONE FLOOR of my throne room, empty but for a single imp who acts as my personal servant. I walked as far as I could before turning around, violently shoving my cloak behind me. I ground my teeth together and cursed Black Annis under my breath, how dare she keep me waiting. My long nails dug furrows into the palm of my other hand. Exquisite pain calmed me enough to think once more.

Narrowing my eyes, I searched out the imp. "Has the Hag arrived yet?"

"No, milord." His voice quivered, as he shrank away from me.

Furious heat swept up my spine. "Where the fuck is she?!"

The imp cowered behind the throne, whimpering.

Lightning struck a feasting table splitting it in half, and when the dust settled Black Annis stood on the splintered remains. She's called a Hag like all of her witch-Fae sisters, but hideous she is not. Pale grey skin, pitch-black hair, and a lithe body made her easy on the eyes. Her name wasn't earned by virtue of her dark features. Black Annis' heart is devoid of anything resembling goodness; she vibrates with malice.

She wore black leather pants and no shirt. Long jeweled necklaces made of diamonds and onyx draped her front covering her breasts. The gems jingled lightly when she walked. Black Annis skirted around me and headed for the throne. She coaxed the imp out from behind the massive chair and sat haphazardly in my seat.

Brazen bitch.

I stormed the dais intent on removing her from my throne. "Watch your insolence, Hag. Remember, I'm the King."

Black Annis threw her head back and cackled, straight black hair spilling over the armrest. "*Are* you the king? Perhaps you should call the *Sluagh* to teach me a lesson in manners." She pouted to mock me before laughing madly.

I halted and sputtered. "You know then?"

The laughing stopped, and her silver eyes bore into my soul. "Did you think I wouldn't feel a shift in power that great?" She spit out.

Rushing the platform, I fell to my knees and begged the Hag. "How do I get it back?"

Black Annis picked at a fingernail carelessly. "You don't, if you're not worthy."

Worthy? I want it now!

I slapped an open palm on the thrones side, jarring her in her seat. "There must be something you can do!"

Raising one foot, Black Annis shoved me away from her and the throne. "I can do many things, for a price."

I bowed my head in penance but my voice was harsh. "Anything, you can have anything."

And once I have my full power back, I'll gut you like the slimy fish you are for forgetting you place.

Her laughter bounced off the walls and crawled around me like a living thing.

"Remember you said that, Corrigan."

Rising Shadows Playlist

My Medicine by The Pretty Reckless

Freak Like Me by Halestorm

Titanium by Madilyn Bailey

Extreme by Valora

Not Strong Enough by Apocalyptica

Oceans by Evanescence

Echoes of an Empire by Picture Me Broken

Carnival of Rust by Poets of the Fall

Never Go Back by Evanescence

Secret Door by Evanescence

Even in Death by Evanesence

When the Darkness Comes by Colbie Callait

Fear by Sarah McLachlan

Running up that hill by Placebo

Amaranthine by Amaranthe

Thank you for reading *Rising Shadows*. I hope that you enjoyed it.

If you can, please write a review so others might give my book a try.

Feel free to contact me on Facebook: facebook.com/bridget.blackwood.9

I love to hear from readers!

Keep reading for the first chapter of book two, *A Scarlet Fury*.

It's Madalaina and Cleary's book!

Preview of
A Scarlet Fury

Book 2 of World of Shadows

by Bridget Blackwood

CHAPTER 1

Madalaina

I GREW UP believing my dad's position as the Alpha Prime made me untouchable. Who'd be stupid enough to mess with me? I mean really! Unfortunately, I didn't rethink my position when my oldest brother Athan went missing, or when my brother Bastien's new mate Rachel exposed a human facility experimenting on non-humans. Too spoiled to think of anyone else, I was angry at my mom for not caring about me and at my dad for putting guards on my tail constantly. I just thought he was overprotective. I slipped the guards every chance I got and it cost me dearly this time.

I'd offered to take Rachel out to shop for last minute baby items; Bastien had been driving her batty with his hovering and she needed a breather. She was due to give birth to my nephew in two weeks, more or less. Rachel wanted to pick up a gift to give her husband and adopted daughter, Livia, after the baby was born. Sure, Bastien made her nuts being overprotective but he loved and supported her. He deserved a pat on the back. For my niece Livia, she bought a 'Big Sis' t-shirt. We'd finished the last of our shopping and carried our bags to her car when I felt something sting my neck. I thought it might've been a bug, but then I plucked out a tiny projectile; cold dread formed a knot in my stomach.

Oh no. Please, no.

I didn't know who drugged me but whatever they planned for me wasn't likely to be pleasant. And what about Rachel and her baby? Would I wake up inside The Richland Institute?

The Richland Institute was a human corporation that secretly experimented on vampires, Therians, and Fae. Therian is the term used to collectively refer to all species of animal shifters. The Richland Institute didn't shy away from human trials either; Rachel was a testament to that. After they'd dosed her with the Arcana virus, Rachel developed telekinetic abilities, enabling her to manipulate the world around her. The Institute had been physically destroyed, but no one ever stepped forward as the mastermind behind the operation. Stuart Richland ran the Institute, but he wasn't the man at the top of the chain. The destruction also brought the existence of beings thought only myth, into the public eye and it had been chaotic ever since.

Rachel and Bastien destroyed The Richland Institute last year.

My muscles went limp and I dropped the bags, falling to the sidewalk. I couldn't move or speak, even breathing was hard. Paralyzed and terrified, I succumbed to the tranquilizer.

Waking up in the pitch darkness alone, my first thought was about Rachel. Was she safe or was she locked in another dark hole like this one? Questions sprung up rapid fire in spite of my head feeling like it was stuffed with cotton.

Where am I? Why would someone kidnap me? Where's Rachel?

I'd panicked when I regained consciousness and screamed my throat raw, then crawled around the perimeter of the blackened room feeling for an exit. I exhausted myself trying to find a way out, I found nothing but a doorknob that wouldn't turn, and gave up. As I laid in the darkness, I did the only thing I could—I used my senses to try and figure out where I was. The damp air reeked of mold and the floor was hard packed dirt. Earlier when searching for an escape, I'd noticed the walls were gritty and felt like rock. The only sounds I could make out were distant footsteps overhead, muffled voices, and the whirring of an industrial air conditioning unit. All these clues led me to believe I was in the basement.

Will I ever see my family again?

Thank god we'd chosen to shop on a school day.

What if we'd waited and taken Livia with us?

I couldn't stand it if something happened to her. Livia was excited to be a big sister and she wanted to be included in everything. Technically, the baby would be her cousin, since she's biologically Athan's daughter.

Screw that. Athan bailed on his family. Bastien and Rachel adopted her, she's their daughter now.

Mom told me I needed to cut Athan some slack after what he went through. The Richland Institute had performed experiments on him and made him do unspeakable things for years while he was their captive. He never met his daughter, Livia, who was also the product of another experiment at Richland. She was half wolf shifter, or Lycan, from her father and half Fae from her mother. She'd been a prisoner of The Richland Institute as well. As a direct member of the Royal Red family line, Amalia, Livia's mother, had been next for the throne behind the Fae Seelie queen. Amalia died after giving birth to Livia. When Athan was freed, he'd learned the fate of his child. He believed himself unfit as a parent and relinquished custody to Bastien and Rachel.

Rachel escaped Richland too. Since getting pregnant, she's tried to keep a lid on her Arcane powers.

Did Rachel use her Arcana to get away?

I doubted she had time to react. I prayed she wasn't locked in another room.

I have no idea how long I sat in the dark. The entire time I'd been in the cell, nobody had brought me food, so when someone threw a bottle of warm water and a loaf of stale bread at me, I focused on my meal. Even with the door open I couldn't have run. Dim light from the hallway streamed in through the open door to light my way, but my eyes were photosensitive from disuse. Maybe I should have tried to escape while the door stood open, but I feared I would slam face first into a wall. I was forced to keep my eyes closed tightly and I couldn't have noticed the guard coming up behind me. If I had use of my sight, I would never have allowed him to get behind me. He hit me with something hard to the back of my head and knocked me out.

I woke up to three men taking turns raping me. They'd moved me from the dark room with the dirt floor to one with smooth grey concrete. The walls were void of any decoration—Just a small boxy space, with only me and a bed as its occupants. The musty scent of sweat, fear, and pain permeated the room and stayed with me long after the men finished. It wouldn't be the last time they assaulted me. I'd tried to fight, but my wrists and ankles were shackled spread eagle to a cast iron bed, and any resistance was met with severe brutality.

I lost count of how many bones they broke. My eyes were nearly swollen shut after repeated punches to my face and I couldn't form words because my jaw was mangled. I don't know which guard used the silver knife on me, but it burned like the fires of hell.

They had no mercy. They stripped me of my clothes and injected me with God knows what. Whoever was in charge of them didn't care what they did. I was raped and beaten over and over again. They fastened an electric dog collar around my neck and took pleasure in watching me jerk from the shocks. An IV kept me hydrated, but no one brought me food,

I don't think I was meant to live long. They'd get whatever they want from me and let me die.

I couldn't shift. The guards said the doctor gave me a shot to suppress my wolf. When I first woke up, I started to change but I couldn't complete the turn. I feared my wolf was gone forever.

Is Rachel okay? Oh god, what about the baby?

I cried all the tears I had to give and now I wanted to die. I couldn't take any more of the torment. The guards realized a broken bone healed in whatever condition it was left in and used the knowledge to their advantage. I knew my rapists by their voices alone. I hadn't gotten a good look at them because the first beating I took was the one to steal my vision. I'd angered them after waking up and trying to throw the man on top of me to the floor. The sadists took a liking to hitting me and it became a game to them. I couldn't escape even if they laid me two inches from the exit. I'd need to crawl on my belly like a snake, but the pain from moving took my breath away. Everything would be better if I died.

Boots on concrete warned me I would soon have guests. I closed my eyes and prayed for peace to rescue me from this hell. I never heard the sound of a door opening or closing so I guessed they didn't bother with it. I wasn't in any condition to get up and walk out so what was the point in security?

A man scolded Rachel. "Do you see what happens when you don't cooperate? Dr. Morris is trying to be nice since you got a brat inside you, but eventually he'll get orders from higher up. You'd be better off if you did what you were told."

Please don't let Rachel see me like this.

I opened my eyes but couldn't make out more than fuzzy

shapes. I recognized her voice though.

"Madalaina, what have they done to you?!"

My mangled jaw and fear prevented me from doing more than making gurgling sounds.

"This is all my fault," she whispered. "Go and tell Morris I'll give him the blood samples *if* he stops hurting her," Rachel ordered through clenched teeth.

I shook my head no, the action sent pain radiating through my body. Conflicted, I wanted the pain to stop but not at the expense of Rachel or the baby. Rachel's shape moved towards me and I did my best to pull away, which caused me tremendous pain.

Gently, she pushed my matted hair off my face and I noted her sharp intake of breath when she scrutinized the extent of the damages to my eyes and mouth. "All you have to do is stay alive, Madalaina. You know they're coming for us."

The guard slapped her hand away and hauled her out of the room. I heard her cursing at them to go to hell.

Guess this visit served its purpose.

The hulking outline of a second guard waited outside the door. He walked in whistling a jaunty tune to himself. I'd learned to fear when they were in an overly good mood because it meant they planned to rape me again. The only blessing was they used condoms. If I survived this, I didn't want a living reminder.

Could I keep a baby if I were pregnant?

I asked myself more than once, but I still didn't know the answer.

Made in the USA
Columbia, SC
28 August 2018